American Scrapbook

ALSO BY JEROME CHARYN

Once upon a Droshky

On the Darkening Green

The Man Who Grew Younger and Other Stories

Going to Jerusalem

American
Scrapbook
Jerome Charyn

THE VIKING PRESS

New York

For Aaron Asher

The natives found it difficult to believe that the earliest travellers had no women with them; for some time they thought that the boys were women. In fact, they were not convinced of their mistake until they satisfied themselves by personal inspection, in which, complains Houtou de Labillardière, they went "much further than we should have expected." However, from the account given by Péron of a similar experience, it seems likely that the natives had a further motive in their curiosity: they wondered whether the white men were made in the same way as themselves. When Péron had induced one of his men to submit to examination, "no sooner had they realized that he was made like them, than they set up all together such loud cries of astonishment and joy that we were deafened."

—THEODORE BESTERMAN,
Men Against Women

American Scrapbook

One

Because even if Lightnings are faster than Grummans I wouldn't fly in an Army plane. I'm going to be a Navy bombardier. And the President will say, Napoleon, Napoleon, I didn't mean what I said about your mother, and he'll have to let her go free. I'll ask him about Chuichi. Will you put my brother in the parachute troops, Mr. President? Will you give him back his uniform and let him fight? And nobody will ever

—Boochie, boochie.

Am not.

—Napoleon, where's your boochie brother? Chuichi the boochie. They don't let no boochies in the American Army.

A-me-me-merican.

—Who gave your sister Ruby her big belly, boochie?

I tried to hit him, but Raymond held my arms, and they took me behind the laundry and dumped me in a bin. The bat on Iggy's flag moved. They wanted to take off my spats, so I kicked and they couldn't hold my feet. The bat moved again. —Napoleon, hold still. We'll put you in head first. He hit me with the flag. I started thinking about sines and cosines, because you can't go to flying school until you pass trigonometry. Why did they have to put Chuichi in the guardhouse when the President

—Ruby Tanaka does it for a nickel or a dime. Any day, any time.

Chuichi caught spiders in the bathhouse and fed them to the bats. I could see Mitsuo coming from the mess hall. —Big Papa, Iggy said. The Bat Patrol ran away. They were all wearing black bandannas. —You tell Big Papa on us, we'll come back and kill you.

Bats have big teeth. And some of them have thumbs. Chuichi hung them up by the tail. Nobody could ever catch a bat. Ruby was afraid of them. She wouldn't make pee when Chuichi put his bats on the wall. Fumi made me take them down. —Id-ee-yut, Mitsuo said. He pulled my hair.

—You have nothing better to do than sit in a barrel all day? Tell Fumiko to take the soap chips out of your hair. And what kind of uniform are you wearing? You look like a saboteur.

—I'm a Sea Scout.

Mitsuo has yellow teeth. —Sea Scout? We live in the middle of a desert. Do you think I gave up my valuable time to bring the Boy Scouts to Manzanar, just so you could mock all of my activities? There are no Sea Scouts here, understand?

—I have my own troop.

He pinched my arm, and I said, Ow, ow, and he wouldn't let go. Why did Fumi have to marry him? Ow. —I do, I do. You can be a single Scout. I wrote the President, and I asked him for permission. You can have your own troop if you want to. The President wouldn't lie.

—I don't have time to listen to your foolishness. Go home.

I saw a dead bat in Mr. Sasaki's outhouse, and I gave it to Chuichi. Chuichi put the bat under his arm and blew on it, and when he picked up his arm the bat moved its wings and flew away. Chuichi, where did you learn how to bring bats back to life? Teach me.

Mitsuo went away.

—Mr. Matsubara.

Whenever he goes for a walk he dreams about his farm, and he can never remember how to get back to the bachelors. Once he tried to crawl under the fence looking for turnips, and a guard almost shot him. You can't blame Mr. Matsubara. It's easy to get lost. If you're ever outside in the middle of a dust storm, you could wander around for a day until the MPs pick you up and take you over to the ministration building. Somebody will feed you crackers and ask you questions. And you'll tell them, Ta-na-ka, Block 38, and they'll laugh and say it aint a fucking spy, it's only Napoleon. I'm not afraid of the Hakujins.

—Mr. Matsubara, do you want to get killed, Mr. Matsubara? You know what will happen if the guard in the tower sees you walking. And the hoodlums will rob your wallet for sure. Chuichi will have to go out at night to get it back. You can't grow turnips here. There's too much dust.

I took him to the bachelors. Nobody paid any attention to us. Dad was playing goh with Mr. Abé.

Dad says all the Nihonjin admirals and generals play goh, and that's why they can beat our admirals and generals. He wants to teach me, but if the War Department ever found out I was studying a Japanese game they wouldn't let me go to flying school. Dad talks about invasions and retreats, but the black and blue stones on the board just sit there all day, and what's the good of having an army if your men can't move? I told him, Dad, Dad, Chuichi wants to see you. And Mitsuo says you can have your own stove. Fumi wants to make a truce with you. Everybody wants you to come back.

I shook his arm, but he wouldn't listen to me. He was too busy.

I could see Ruby's bloomers behind the curtain, and I didn't want to peek, so I put my knuckles over my eyes, but the light still came through. Mitsuo was snoring.

Harold came in, and he took off his pea coat and his shoes, and he got into bed. He sleeps with his shirt and his pants on, because Mitsuo won't let anybody light the stove after midnight. —Hal, I said, do you think Sam is ever going to fight again? But Fumi said, Shhh, Mitsuo is sleeping. So I got up, put the blanket over my shoulders, and walked over to Harold's bed. This time I whispered. —Won't they need bantamweights after the war? He said no. —How come, Harold? Sam Yoshima was the best bantamweight in the world before the war. You said so. Didn't he fight in Hollywood? Didn't he beat Little Pancho? Maybe his headaches will go away if he stays in the shade. And the way he punches, he won't need more than one good eye. Do you want me to be Spider Sam's sparring partner, Hal? I'll train him every day. I swear. Fumi gave me dirty looks, so I went back to bed. Harold fell asleep, and I could hear Mr. and Mrs. Sugimoto snore through the walls. Snores are like fingerprints. Mitsuo's snores are easiest to tell. He whistles through his nose, and he rests a minute between every snore. Fumi's snores are quiet. You couldn't tell she was sleeping unless you listened hard. Ruby never snores. That's because she stays up all night. After everybody falls asleep she puts on her record player and does the boogie-woogie. She dances in her bloomers. Sometimes Wendell visits her at night. He comes in through the window. Wendell sells dirty cards to the old bachelors, and if you're his friend he'll give you a scum bag for free. If you wear it overnight, it's supposed to make your pecker grow. Wendell wears one all the time. The door slammed, and the chair fell over. Mitsuo grunted, and he woke up. He rubbed his eyes. —Who makes so much noise? Chuichi was standing near the door. He was wearing his combat boots, and the scarf that Fumi made for him. —Who's there?

—It's only me, Big Papa, Chuichi said. Only me.

—Who dares talk to me that way? You, brother-in-law, you? You were with that Kibei bastard Toshio, weren't you? Making trouble. Staying out late. You're drunk too. On Toshio's filthy saké. Troublemakers. Bastards. I'll throw you all out of my block.

Fumi tried to Shhh him. —You'll wake Harold. And Napoleon.

—I'll wake the whole camp if I want. Who's block manager here, me or him? Mitsuo stood up on the bed. —Who, who? His feet sank into the mattress, and the bed went up and down.

—Tosh didn't put us in here, remember that, Big Papa.

—You shut up. I know he's planning trouble. You'll all end up in the stockade. Kibei bastard, he wants the Japs to win the war. We're Americans here, understand? Fumiko, tell him, tell him what will happen to all of us if he makes trouble.

Fumiko told Chuichi to get undressed, and she made Mitsuo lie down again. Mitsuo pulled his blanket over his face. —I don't want to look at him. He makes me sick.

I made room for Chuichi. I wanted to ask him about the Navy Air Force, but I knew Mitsuo would shout at me. Chuichi took off his clothes. He always sleeps that way, even in the winter. Chuichi growled, so I hunched up in one corner of the bed. Chuichi, why does Toshio say prayers to the Emperor like all the old yabos? Wasn't he born in America? Just because he went to high school in Japan it doesn't mean he has to follow all the Nihonjin customs.

Mom, Chuichi is mad at everybody, Ruby hides in her little room, Harold is busy with the *Patriot*, Mitsuo won't let me wear my uniform, and Dad is living with the bachelors because he says Fumi tries to boss him around. It's cold in Montana. Do you have a warm coat? Mom, you know Wendell, Mr. Haraguchi's nephew, he is going to run away from Manzanar, and he wants me to come with him. I told him what the FBI did to you, and he is making plans to help you escape from Montana. Mitsuo calls Wendell a hoodlum because of his zoot suit, but Wendell is a better American than anybody. Mom, I can send you my pea coat, and I'll put some coal in the pockets. I read Harold's articles. He says all the senators in California are crazy, but we have to show people that we aren't spies and saboteurs. Mitsuo thinks

Toshio Yasuda is the Emperor's stooge. Chuichi would never be friends with a spy. Mom, do you think Dad would live with us again if Fumi went to the bachelors and talked to him? Harold could put up another curtain, and he could have his own room. And he wouldn't have to come out unless he wanted to take a walk or play shogi with

—Scamp, Fumi said, why aren't you in school?

—I'm thinking, I'm thinking about what I'm going to say when I write Mom a letter.

—Letters? Nobody can read your scribbles. Mother would tear your hair out if she knew you were a truant. Go to school.

So I went outside, but I didn't go to school. Mrs. Hildegaard is bald and deaf, and sometimes she gets asthma attacks. She's too old to teach in a Hakujin school, and that's why they brought her to Manzanar. All she ever talks about is Patrick Henry and Nathan Hale. Nathan's a kuichi name. Wendell told me. Nathan Hale was a kike. He had nine brothers and sisters, and he fucked them all in the fields. But that's not in the history book, so why go to school? Wendell fucks all the girls behind the grandstand. That's why he needs so many scum bags. He made Ruby's belly big, but I won't tell, I won't tell, I won't tell.

—I'm going to walk through the Provost Marshal's

gate wearing an MP's uniform. And nobody's going to stop me.

All the zootsuiters laughed. —Wendell, who's going to give you an MP's uniform?

—You dumbbells. Did you ever know anything I wanted that I couldn't get? I'll trade with the guards. First I'll get a hat, then shoes, then an arm band, and pretty soon I'll have a uniform. I could get all the arm bands I want for one pussy tickler. I'll bet Frisco Jap-town is filled with niggers now. And all the noodle shops are closed.

—You going to Frisco? Masao said. Frisco's three hundred miles away.

—So what? With my arm band, I could stop any car on the highway. You can get arrested for refusing to give a ride to an MP. And when I get to town I won't need no uniform. I'll wear a China button. If people start giving me suspicious looks, I'll sing them a song about Madam Chiang Kai-shek. And don't think I'm going to get a schoolboy job. I'm not leaving camp just to become a coolie. I'm going to sell souvenirs on Grant. And if anybody tries to steal my corner I'll brain them with a rock. Come on.

—Where we going, Wendell?

—To the canteen. Wendell pointed to me. —Him too.

—I'm not going if Napoleon's going.

—Shut up, Wendell said, and I trailed behind him.

The Bat Patrol was holding maneuvers near the fire-break, and when they saw Wendell they froze. Masao wanted to steal their flags, but Wendell said, I aint in the mood. I saw Iggy shiver.

Wherever Wendell walks, the women grab their children and the old men get out of his way. Mitsuo wants the Nihonjin camp police to shave Wendell's head and take away his zoot suit, but the Nihonjin police are afraid of him. And the Provost Marshal can't do anything unless Wendell commits a crime against the United States. When we went into the canteen the men and women turned around and whispered, and a few of the high-school girls came over. They said, Wendell dance with me, because Wendell is the jitterbug king of Manzanar, but Wendell said he was busy and he walked up to the counter. —Service, he said, and he knocked on the counter. Mr. Wakayama, the canteen manager, was selling licorice to the bachelors, but when Wendell knocked he came right over. Wendell pulled me close to him, and he said, Wakayama, Napoleon wants cherry licorice, Joya, Fifth Avenue, nigger babies, and candy corn.

—No Joya today, Mr. Wakayama said. No Fifth Avenue, no nigger baby.

—Wakayama, you got them in the back. We can't have a party without nigger babies.

Mr. Wakayama grumbled and called us bandits and pigs in Japanese, but he still went inside his storeroom.

Wendell whistled, and the zootsuiters reached over the counter and stuffed my pockets with Baby Ruth and Turkish Delight. —Go, Wendell said, and he pushed me toward the door. Mr. Wakayama came running out. —Thief, thief, he screamed, help, murder, thief. The bachelors glared at me and raised their fists, and the women hissed, and I didn't know if I should run, or stay, or fight the bachelors, or give the candy away, and meanwhile Masao tripped me and I tumbled into the bachelors, and the candy spilled out of my pockets. The bachelors pinched me and kicked me and held me prisoner for Mr. Wakayama, and all the time I heard Wendell laugh. Mr. Wakayama slapped me. —Scum, pig. You rob from your people and you expect Mitsuo to take you out of trouble.

He slapped me again, and Wendell came over. He wasn't laughing any more. Mr. Wakayama quieted down. —Who said anything about stealing, Wendell said. I'm paying for everything. He stared at the bachelors, and they crawled around on their knees and picked up every candy bar. Wendell took out his money pouch, untied the leather strings, and put eleven nickels in Mr. Wakayama's hand. —Apologize to Napoleon. Wendell put his hands on his hips. —I want everybody here to apologize. You first. Mr. Wakayama mumbled something and bowed his head.

—What's that? Wendell said. I'm deaf in one ear.

—Very sorry, Mr. Wakayama said, and he bowed

again. Then the bachelors bowed, and the high-school girls, and the women and their children. Wendell made the zootsuiters bow, and then we all walked out.

Whhhhhhsh, whhhhhhsh, listen to the wind. The door knocks, the windows rattle, and the bedbugs drop from the walls. Bats are blind, and I could catch them in my shirt, but Chuichi wouldn't care. Chuichi has the scabies. The bedbugs won't leave him alone. Every morning I have to shake them out of my spats. Lice are worse than scabies. When we lived in Watsonville, Ruby had to shave her hair. Dad trapped the bedbugs and kept them in a bottle under the sink. The FBI thought it was contraband. They came at night and opened Mom's drawers. They found the Emperor's picture and Chuichi's broken flashlight, and they tore open the mattresses and left the stuffing on the floor. My brother's a soldier, I told them, he's fighting for the USA, and they said they were sorry, but they took Mom with them and the bedbugs in the bottle, and Dad sat on the floor and cried. Dad, Dad, come to bed, we'll rescue Mom in the morning. Chuichi wouldn't let them take her away. Dad. Fee fi fo, I smell the blood of a boochieman. Japs are worth a dollar a pound. Ruby hid her boyfriend in the outhouse. I saw the blood on her bloomers. Mitsuo says the Nisei are Amerijaps. What am I? Catch Napoleon by his toe, and if he hollers, drown him. I don't want to be the man without a country. I'll be a bandit. I'll go with Wendell.

But if you steal during wartime it's worse than sabotage. I'll be a bedbug and bite Mitsuo.

—Napoleon, Napoleon, Napoleon.
—I heard you, I said.
—So why don't you answer?
—Because I'm doing trigonometry.
—But you never go to school.
—I'm studying on my own.
—Take me to hear Toshio.
—It's dinnertime. Tosh is in the kitchen.
—No he's not. He's speaking in the laundry room. Take me.

Ruby doesn't like to go any place by herself because the old women spit at her and the little children make Shame, Shame. I have to protect her. —How do you know he's speaking in the laundry?
—Wendell told me.
—We'll miss dinner. And Fumi will think we're out making trouble.

Ruby tickled me and sat on my chest, and I said, I'll take you, lemme go. I made her wait. —I have to put on my spats.

—Hurry, hurry, she said, but I sat on the bed. —You know I never go outside without my spats. So she leaned over and helped me lace them up, and then she took my hand and pushed me outside.

Mitsuo says Toshio's a Fascist, because he makes

speeches against the ministration. But before Toshio worked in the kitchen the food was terrible. We had Spam every day for weeks, there were always bugs in the potatoes, the spoons were never clean, and sometimes the cooks peed in the soup. Now all the Hakujin workers want to eat with us. On Sundays Toshio makes rice cakes for the children and sushi for the bachelors. And the zootsuiters never make noise in the mess hall. Toshio would throw them out.

Toshio has a bozo haircut like the Japanese soldiers, and if you see him from far away he looks bald.

—Colonists? Toshio said. Do colonists need barbed wire and watchtowers and machine guns? Brothers, make no mistakes. We are here for the duration. Your children will grow up here, and they will die here.

The laundry room was crowded with women and children, but there were only a few men. The men stood near the door with their hands in their pockets. Chuichi was with them, but he didn't say hello. The women were very busy. They leaned over the washtubs, scrubbed bloomers, blouses, and long johns, and listened to Toshio. The children played under the tubs. A man stuck his head through the door and shouted at Toshio. —You stinking Jap. Go back to Tokyo. Then he ran out. I didn't recognize him. He wasn't from our block.

Toshio talked and talked, but I watched Chuichi. He was biting his lip. —Vanish, Toshio said. No more Issei, no more Nisei, no more Sansei in America. One by one the women picked up their washboards, found their kids under the tubs, and left. They passed by us, but they made believe Ruby wasn't there. The men stayed near the door.

Toshio scowled, and the scowl made marks on his forehead. Then he laughed, and the marks disappeared. He took his apron and his baker's hat out of a bag, and he put them on. The baker's hat looks like a mushroom. Toshio bowed to the men and the women who were still in the laundry room. Then we all followed him out. —Bean soup tonight, he said. He had to hold on to his hat to keep the wind from knocking it off. The dust blew around him, and all I could see was the big mushroom on his head.

Mr. Matsubara won't be looking for turnips any more. Yesterday a guard shot off his head. Wendell says he saw the head float over the grandstand, but I don't believe him. The Hakujin police took Mr. Matsubara's body away, and nobody knows where it is. Toshio marched in front of the ministration building with a sign. It said, NO MORE GUNS AT MANZANAR. SOLDIERS, SHOOT YOURSELVES. The MPs came and tore up Toshio's sign, and they put him in jail. The cooks didn't know what to do. We had string beans for breakfast and string beans for lunch. Mitsuo had a meeting. Everybody in our block was there. He stood on a box and shouted at us. —Is Mitsuo your manager? Was he not appointed to look out for all your rights? Who will believe in this Mitsuo if he allows the white faces to arrest one of his constituents?

The old yabos cheered, and the women cried, and Mitsuo sent a delegation to the Provost Marshal, and he went to see the Camp Director. The next day Toshio showed up in the kitchen wearing his baker's hat. We clapped until Toshio stood on a table and made a speech. Toshio cursed the Hakujins, and Mitsuo walked out of the mess hall, but everybody was nice to Ruby. Nobody spit at her.

I saw Mr. Matsubara's head in a dream. It had blood all over it, and it asked me a question. —Napoleon, who are you, Napoleon? I didn't know what to say.

—Mr. Matsubara, if I put a penny in your eye it's supposed to bring good luck. But Mr. Matsubara didn't want any pennies. I must have shouted, because Chuichi poked me, and I woke up.

Fumi came over. —What's wrong with you?

—Nothing, I said. I had a talk with Mr. Matsubara's head.

—How old are you, Sam?

—Forty-two.

—When were you born?

—1915.

I started counting on my fingers, and I said, Spider Sam, how can you be forty-two? Don't you know arithmetic? If you take sixteen years away from 1942, you only get twenty-five years. You must be twenty-five.

Sam has scars on his head, and it's hard to see his eyes.

—I'm forty-two.

Harold told me never to argue with Sam, because it only makes his head hurt more, so I didn't say anything. We passed the factories, and I could see the girls hunching over their sewing machines. They're making coats and camouflage nets for the Navy. The spools went around and around, and the machines made so much noise I thought all the girls must be deaf. If Sam's forty-two, how is he going to make a comeback?

Harold can't print his articles in the *Patriot* unless he shows them to the Camp Director, and sometimes he lets me and Sam bring the articles over. We have to walk across camp until we get to the factories and the hospital. The Hakujins live behind the hospital. The MPs and the camp police were playing baseball in their field.

—Sam, why don't you become a wrestler? Toshio will feed you until you get fat, and then you can bump anybody with your belly. All the sumo champions will be afraid of you.

Sam spit on the ground when I mentioned Toshio.

—I hate the Kibei. They make trouble.

One of the MPs pointed his bat at us and laughed, and Sam walked behind me. He didn't want the MPs to see him.

A Hakujin worker stopped us near the ministration building. He asked us who we were and where we were going. I told him our names and our block numbers. I showed him Harold's articles. —We have to see the Director.

He told us not to take any flowers from the Hakujin garden, and not to bother the children, and he said we should do our business and leave.

Sam said, Yes Sir, but I was mad. —Who wants your flowers? My brother works for the *Patriot*, and I go wherever he tells me to go. The MPs heard me shout at him, and they said to the Hakujin, Don't you know Napoleon? He's the commander of the Sea Scouts.

The Camp Director wasn't in his office, and we had to leave the articles with his secretary. She made us tea and gave us crackers and jam. Sam spilled tea on his pants, and I had to wipe him with my handkerchief. The secretary looked and looked at Sam, and then she said, I know you. Aren't you Spider Yoshima? I saw you fight at the Hollywood Legion. You were wonderful. She called over the other secretaries. Sam spilled his tea again. I knew what he wanted. We sneaked out of the ministration building.

I went to school today. It was cold sitting in bed, and the wind was making too much noise. Ruby was busy painting her toenails, and I had nobody to play checkers with, so I went to school. When I came in everybody said, Napoleon's here, and Mrs. Hildegaard gave me some paper and told me to write a composition about America. That was our topic for the day. But when I asked her what I should write about America, she Shhhed me and said I was disturbing the class. —Isn't Manzanar America? She came over to my desk. —Napoleon Tanaka, you are a lazy, unruly boy. Do you want to remain in the eighth grade for your whole life? Write whatever comes to mind.

I wrote about Chuichi. And when it came my turn to read the composition I told the class how Chuichi could have won the Purple Heart if the parachute troops would have taken him, and how the President made a mistake. I cursed the Army and all the congressmen, and Mrs. Hildegaard took my composition away and called me disrespectful, so I walked out.

I went to the grandstand and climbed to the top. Nobody was around. I made a windshield with my hands, and I could see all the barracks and the firebreaks. I tried to look for our block, but I couldn't find it. Smoke was coming from the factories, and the siren on the ministration building went off.

Whhhooooeeeeeeeeeeeeeeeeeeeeeeeeeeeeeeeeeeeeee

Mrs. Hildegaard, if I could take that siren and wind it up so it went louder and louder, and then shout into it, maybe my mother could hear me in Montana. I would say, MOM, DONNNNNN WORRRRRRRREEEE BOUUUUUUU MEEEEEEE ANNNNNN CHHHHHHHHUUUWEECHEEEEE

T*wo*

Statement to United States Army and War Relocation Authority, signed by Mitsuo Arimoto, November 8, 1942

I, Mitsuo Arimoto, formerly vice-president of the Watsonville chapter of the Japanese-American Citizens League, and presently manager of Block Number 38 at the Manzanar Relocation Center, make the following statement to Colonel F. Charles Gripp, Provost Marshal, and Cleveland Swann, Project Director. I have not been coerced in any way to make this statement, and I know that it can be used against me in a court of law.

On November 1, Monroe Beardsly, Assistant Project Director, informed me that Senator Gary Bone of the California Legislature would be arriving at Manzanar on November 7 to investigate conditions at the center, and that he would be visiting my block. Assistant Director Beardsly further informed me that Senator Bone was highly critical of the center's aims and operations, that he had on numerous occasions denounced the entire relocation program on the floor of the Senate and had accused the War Relocation Authority of mollycoddling evacuees and of providing a breeding ground for Fascists and Communists, and that he wanted the Army to have greater control over the internal organization of Manzanar. Assistant Director Beardsly believed that once Senator Bone saw the actual operations of the center, he would no longer be antagonistic to the program and would report back favorably to the Legislature.

In order to facilitate Senator Bone's investigation, Assistant Director Beardsly called a general meeting of all Caucasian and evacuee personnel. Alexander Cremin, Chief Steward, proposed that all known agitators be confined the evening before Senator Bone's arrival. Several of the block managers, including myself, argued against Steward Cremin's proposal. We felt that a general roundup of evacuees might precipitate riots and flare-ups, which would prevent Senator Bone from moving freely throughout the center and would ultimately damage the evacuee cause. Block managers Osaka and Murakami made a counterproposal. They suggested that all managers report back to their block councils, that the councils impress upon evacuees the importance of Senator Bone's visit, and that the councils themselves police all areas during Senator Bone's stay at Manzanar. This proposal was voted upon and approved by the overwhelming majority of all personnel present.

I carried out the proposal of managers Osaka and Murakami to the best of my ability, and I can personally vouch for the loyalty of each and every council member and evacuee of Block Number 38. Therefore I cannot at this time fully account for the riot that ensued in my block during Senator Bone's visit. Senator Bone in no way provoked this disturbance, nor did he contribute to its inception. This senseless riot occurred in the mess hall. While Senator Bone ate with us, certain agitators entered the mess hall via the garbage-disposal area, knocked over tables and chairs, and began hurling food at evacuees. Fortunately Senator Bone was unharmed. Council members and evacuee police surrounded Senator Bone and prevented the rioters from approaching him. I estimate the damage to the mess hall to be $40. I did not recognize any of the rioters and am convinced that they came from another block.

The foregoing statement was made at the request of Assistant Director Beardsly, and I solemnly swear that it is to the best of my knowledge wholly true and correct.

(signed) Mitsuo Arimoto

Witnesses:

F. CHARLES GRIPP, US ARMY

CLEVELAND SWANN, WRA

They come in committees of one, two, and three, with petitions, with complaints, and I have to mend, wheedle, and steal for them. There's no toilet paper in the women's latrine. The bachelors want another tub. The nurse won't prescribe a new remedy for Mr. Suboto's gout, and I have to battle the health service for him. Mrs. Harada's daughters monopolize the ironing boards, and nobody else can get work done. And Mr. Iké's here with his own complaint. He argues like a true scholar: if the women's crap pots have partitions and stalls, why must the men be denied? Are they any less shy than the women? This lack of privacy is causing him great harm. It interferes with his bowel movements. I have told him, "Mr. Iké, I am negotiating with Block 17. Do you think lumber is easy to come by? Don't worry, you will have your partitions and doors. I will notify you when the lumber arrives." Does he listen? He comes to my office every morning and sits on the bench. He doesn't have to say a single word. His presence is enough of an accusation. Iké, I am not responsible for the sensibility of your bowels. I make faces at him, I frown. It does no good. He sits. I send out my assistant, Hiroshi. "Get me lumber, this instant. I have things on my mind." He comes back with empty hands. "Boss, you can't even get a toothpick." I send him out again. "You miserable, I'll cripple you for life." Hiroshi is not as stupid as he looks. My anger doesn't offend him in the least. He's used to my ways. He knows I am simply putting on a show for the petitioners in my office. "Lout, lumber I say." I allow my eyes to pop out. "Lumber." I have long ago learned the magical properties of a shout. How else would I survive as block manager? If you shout in the right way, long enough and loud enough, people begin to think that you are getting things done and they stop pestering you for a little while. Let Iké sit; today I have other problems.

I head for the bachelors' dorm. It's always a madhouse in there. The old men fight, pick their noses, show off their new pajamas, sing dirty songs. The stench is unbearable. You would need a gas mask to remain immune to the sweat, the farts, the sour breath emanating from every bed. There are no brothels at Manzanar, and the old men have to relieve themselves under the covers.

The bachelors crowd around me with their requests. Mr. Wanatabe wants to sue Sears Roebuck. They sent him the wrong size underwear through the mail. Mr. Kumagai is having trouble with his teeth. "See me in my office, please. Citizens, my assistant will file all your complaints. Action will be taken in due time." I have business with Uncle Haraguchi. He's sitting on his bed, reading one of his Fascist pamphlets. He has free reign in the dorm. Haraguchi was a bigwig in the Black Dragon Society before the war. How he escaped being interned only the Emperor knows! Fumiko's mother was a poor history teacher at Buddhist school, and the FBI carted her away. I'm sure Haraguchi has a short-wave radio hidden somewhere in the dorm. He sees me, but he goes right on reading his pamphlet.

"*Citizen,*" I say, modulating my voice for the proper tone. You have to be cagey with Haraguchi. He looks up.

"Citizen, you heard my speech at the block meeting. Senator Bone of the Legislature will be here tomorrow. I am familiar with your ideas. I respect them. Your attachment to the mother country is honorable. But this is not the way it will seem to the Senator. He may want to visit the dorm. I ask you beforehand not to challenge his views."

He smiles at me like a monkey.

"Citizen, I am responsible for every living soul in this block. I can have the dormitory watched. Would you prefer to have a white policeman on guard inside the door? It is within my power to do so."

His monkey face doesn't change, but I know my words have hit home. How could he tune in Tokyo with the camp police around? But you cannot push him too far. If his radio were taken away he would just as soon spend the rest of his days in Swann's jail. He puts down the pamphlet and crosses his arms. "Mitsuo, let the Senator make his visit. I will sit here. We have nothing in common. And if you bring your white policeman down on my head, I will teach myself to play knock rummy with him. It will be no misfortune for me."

"Uncle, I am no fonder of the camp police than you are. I ask only two things of you. Don't interfere with Senator Bone. And curb Wendell."

He picks up his pamphlet. I've angered him, but it can't be helped.

"*Sensei*, I know you are not responsible for your

nephew's behavior, but one of his pranks could ruin everything for us. Bone will make sure that whatever few privileges we have will be taken away. The MPs will be everywhere."

Haraguchi has stopped listening. I would leave the dorm this minute, but the bachelors are great promoters of customs and courtesies, and they would be grievously offended if I did not say hello to my honorable father-in-law. I am feuding with the old man. He has made Fumiko's life miserable. He has insulted me in public. But if I walked past his bed the bachelors would swarm my office demanding apologies. It would undermine their faith in me. Little Father, you will have your hello from me, but no more. The old man has abandoned goh today. He's looking at dirty picture cards with his cronies. He flips the queen of spades. The bachelors are very brazen about the cards. The camp police have stopped confiscating them. What good would it do? Wendell has flooded the market.

"Father, how is your health today?"

His face wrinkles up. "Go away, Mitsuo, go away."

The other bachelors laugh.

"Father, if you prefer living here, you might at least visit us once in a while."

He's through with the queen. He picks up another card. "Mitsuo, you are standing in the light. Go away."

The bachelors laugh again. I've said enough to satisfy all proprieties, and now I'm free to walk out.

Hiroshi is waiting for me. He blows on his hands to keep them warm. He's impatient, my Hiroshi. He wants to flirt with the factory girls. Maybe they'll give him some hemp, which he'll twist into little figures and sell to grandmothers outside the canteen. I'm interfering with his profits.

"Boss, your brother wants to see you."

I grab him by his collar and give him a shake. "I have no brothers in this world. Say brother again and your brains will be on the floor."

He corrects himself. "Brother-in-law, brother-in-law."

"Which one?"

"Harold." He starts to run away.

"You," I say. "Find Toshio for me. Have him outside Harold's office in half an hour."

He curses me under his breath.

"Ingrate," I tell him. "Conduct your business affairs on your own time."

He answers with a shrug. "What if Toshio doesn't want to come? If I bother him, his cooks will chop me to pieces."

"Donkey, remember, you are Mitsuo's assistant. Nobody will touch you. Now go."

What commodity is he selling today? Perfume some guard smuggled into camp for him? Hair tonic? Every stud at Manzanar owes him money. My brother wants to see me, ha! What does he know? He has a mother. He has a father. Two brothers. Two sisters. Uncles, aunts, cousins at Tule, at Gila, at Topaz, at Heart Mountain, everywhere. It must cost the United States a fortune just to feed his family alone. Should I tell you about my family, Hiroshi?

I hear a noise. The sound is unmistakable. Raymond is making music on his crumpled tuba. The Boy Scouts are practicing for tomorrow. I had to come up with instruments for them. A discarded drum from an old Army band, a tuba with a damaged bell that belongs to one of the stewards, a triangle from the kindergarten class, and a harmonica that I've had for twenty years. Mitsuo's ensemble. The boys are near the women's latrine. Raymond has never played the tuba before; he tries his best. The others are clowning around. They bump one another with the drum, they dig the triangle into one another's ribs, they take turns spitting into the harmonica. "Ignatius Shibuya, I'll break your head." The boys come to attention. Ignatius wipes the spittle from the harmonica. LeRoy polishes the triangle on his pants. Kenny hugs the drum. I parade in front of them. "Is this the way a welcoming committee is supposed to behave? Am I paying you to perform tricks?" I glare at them. They begin to whine. "Mitsuo, Mitsuo, don't take our instruments away." The women pause outside the latrine to watch us. LeRoy raps the triangle once with his puny silver hammer. Kenny gets busy with his drum. Raymond puffs out his cheeks.

"Play and sing," I order them.

They bang, they scratch, they blow on their instruments, and sing for me:

> Senator, Senator, we welcome you to Manzanar.
> Greetings from the Bats.
> Yah! Yah! Yah!

"Again," I say, appraising each instrument. I rap on Kenny's drum, I peer inside the tuba, I guide LeRoy's hammer, I show Ignatius how to breathe. I give the four of them a nickel apiece and tell them to practice for an hour. Bored by the sounds, the women line up inside the latrine.

Harold's typewriter and mimeo machine are idle. His reporters are out scouting for news; his two secretaries hover around him. He dismisses them when he sees me. His eyes smart behind his spectacles.

He hisses at me.

"Are you ill, Harold? What's wrong?"

"You know what's wrong. Someone was in here last night tampering with my mimeograph. Mitsuo, you are an unprincipled, miserable bastard. You told Swann not to okay my article on Bone. And Beardsly took care of the rest."

I walk slowly around his desk. "What do I care about your articles! Am I Swann's censor? Who says he didn't okay it?"

"He hasn't sent it back. He's stalling until Bone comes

and goes. You put him up to it. Those are your methods, Mitsuo."

"Give him credit for more brains, Harold. I had nothing to do with it. If Bone saw your article he would send a dozen committees down on us. Swann knows it. We all know it."

Harold begins to twitch. "All I hear is Bone, Bone." He flails his arms, and the dust flies. "Crackpots come in and out of here every day, and nobody pays the slightest attention. Ministers who want to save our souls. Reporters who are ready to prove that there are bacchanals in the mess halls every night, orgies in the latrines, that we're poisoning the water, fouling the air, that we're all a bunch of spies and perverts, Swann included. So why is everybody so worried about Bone?"

He takes off his spectacles and gets up from his chair. He prefers myopia to me. "What more can they do to us, Mitsuo? Starve us to death? Take us out and shoot us?"

"Things could be worse, Harold." Blind, he stumbles across the room. "For Christ's sake, put on your specs! Beardsly has promised us. As soon as the war fever is over we will all be getting leave clearances. That's why we have to be careful. One investigation, and everything will be ruined."

He sits down. "What did I say, Mitsuo? Was it propaganda? Lies? Didn't Bone help organize the Home

Front Commandos?" He fumbles through his desk, swears, and pulls out a notebook with legal-sized paper. He holds the notebook under his nose, turns one page, and reads to me: "*The Jap represents the greatest possible threat to our country. There is no such thing as a loyal Jap. His only allegiance is to his Emperor. The Jap is cowardly; the Jap is cruel.*"

I grab the notebook and tear out pages at random. "Do you think I am a fool? I have heard his speeches, Harold. I am not unaware of his racist filth. Should I join forces with Toshio Yasuda? Should I badger Bone when he arrives? Kill him? And what would happen here? Martial law. We would be branded like cattle. You wanted a newspaper. You have one now. Don't be so eager to give it up."

He gets up again and puts on his spectacles; they sit crookedly on his nose. He points his finger at me. "Mitsuo, I feel sorry for you. You won't have your way with Bone no matter how many accommodations you make. You will dance for him, and he will laugh at you. All your contortions, all the wonders you have planned, will come to nothing. People will talk when they see you standing too near the Senator. He will run from here scot-free, and in the end you will have to pay."

"Harold, I don't give a damn. I have my block to worry about."

I leave him scrunched up between his typewriter and mimeograph machine, the notebook in his lap. His secretaries immediately reappear. They twitter when they pass me. I, Mitsuo, renounce all relatives through marriage. The Tanakas have wicked tongues.

Hiroshi comes running across the firebreak. I measure my curses. Hiroshi will only take so much abuse.

"*Baboon.*"

He stops.

"I told you to bring Toshio."

"Boss, he wouldn't come."

"What do you mean, wouldn't come? Why didn't he put someone else in charge of his kitchen?"

"He wasn't in the kitchen, Mitsuo. He's in the latrine. He was very surly. He said that if you want him you know where to find him."

"He dared talk that way? Were others present?"

"Yes. A few bachelors and a cook."

"Hiroshi, take my answer to him. Tell him I'll meet him halfway. Between barracks."

He pulls in his shoulders. "Mitsuo, I asked him twice. He won't budge from the shithouse." His head bobs nervously; Hiroshi cannot bear to stand still.

"Dolt, run. You have my permission. You're dismissed for the day."

Kicking up dust clouds, he's on his way. To the canteen? To one of the washrooms? Hiroshi has business everywhere. His life is one continual stream of buying, selling, and storing.

Toshio is squatting in the latrine. All the seats are occupied except one. Toshio has saved it for me. The flies buzz overhead, the spiders travel on the floor, the bachelors strain on their pots. Young men, old men, peek in, mill around for a minute, go out. I stand over Toshio. He looks the other way. He is out to humiliate me. He won't do business unless I squat down next to him and take off my pants. "Toshio Yasuda, I am a busy man." The bachelors look up. I have no alternatives today. I sit down. Toshio offers me a cup of his home-made saké. His cooks have brewed it for him in the kitchen. I take the cup. If the Caucasian police found us with the saké we would all be arrested. The bachelors grin at me. I drink. "Toshio, I saved you once from a long vacation in jail. I won't be able to do it again. My powers are limited."

Okazaki, Toshio's second cook in command, taunts me from his pot near the corner. "Big Papa, we all know you are the white father's number-one boy. The great white father Swann would not dream of wiping his ass without first consulting you."

The bachelors laugh raucously and poke one another, but Toshio sits with his hands on his knees.

"Toshio, whatever differences there are between us, I ask you to end your war against the administration for one day. No speeches, no politics, while the Senator is here. I ask you this for your own good."

It is Toshio's turn to laugh. He leans back and slaps his thighs. The bachelors ape him.

Iké is right. I must find wood for partitions and doors. A block manager cannot conduct his affairs sitting in an open latrine.

"Toshio, there has been talk of a roundup. Listen to me. Beardsly will find room for every troublemaker in the colony."

He shakes his head. "*Mitsuo-kun*, if Beardsly hides us, if he throws us underground, we will jabber, we will bark, we will howl, we will make such noise that the good people of Inyo County will think there has been an eruption in hell. The Senator will die of fright." He digs his fists into his sides. "Do not come here with your threats. You will get no promises from me."

"Toshio, do you have nothing more to say?"

He gets up, unrolls the toilet paper with much ceremony, wipes, waits for Okazaki, and walks out together with him, stepping between the spiders.

"Toshio, is this your final word?"

I glare at the bachelors. They sit on their pots like magpies.

Certainly, we need partitions and doors. I will have to trade with Block 17. After tomorrow. Hiroshi will handle it. Lumber for light bulbs.

It rained all morning. Beardsly sat with us in the little shack near the main gate and cursed the sky. He was wearing his pith helmet, and he kept hiking up his poncho and peering at his logbook. He meant to assure us with his wealth of facts. "The annual precipitation of the entire Owens Valley is under two inches. The last time it rained here was in May. It must be a mistake." He grimaced, peeked outside. The rain made a loud clatter on the roof of his helmet. It was damp and stifling in the shack, and we stood around him, four block managers, two stewards, three policemen, and an aide, shoulder to shoulder, with no room to maneuver or breathe. I was the first to leave. "Boy Scouts," I mumbled. "Have to warm up the band."

I ran over to my office. Thank God, no one was there. I slept for an hour and then rounded up the band. Kenny had an upset stomach. I had to promise his mother not to keep him out in the rain too long. We waited on her porch until the Senator's party approached, and then we assembled hurriedly on the firebreak. Kenny dropped his drum. The tuba filled with water, and when Raymond went to blow, the bell started gurgling.

It didn't really matter. The Senator stopped us in the middle of our song. "Gentlemen," he said, "I'm deeply grateful for your welcome. But I didn't come to Manzanar for parades and song fests." He wasn't wearing a hat, and Beardsly, who was holding an umbrella over the Senator's head and looking very glum, had to keep in step with him. The Senator brought his aides, and behind him were delegations from Blocks 9, 17, and 27. The councilmen wore paper banners indicating their block numbers and locations; the banners were already soaked. After we were introduced, the Senator dismissed Beardsly and all the delegations, grabbed my arm, and said, "Mitsuo, I want to mix, I want to mingle." He pointed sadly to Beardsly. "No guided tours. Show me your block, Mitsuo."

Bewildered, the boys picked up their song.

——Bats.
Yah! Yah! Yah!

Beardsly stayed behind holding the umbrella. The Senator's aides followed us for a few steps, but he quickly waved them away. He was blunt with them. "Amuse yourselves. Scram."

I didn't know what to say; he was holding my arm very tight.

"Senator Bone, you had better come out of the rain."

"What?" he said, squinting at me. "I wanted to come here in disguise. Everybody tightens up when they know who you are. But it would have had repercussions. The Army isn't enthusiastic about illegal entries. Mitsuo, show me everything. I want to see the colony. We'll start here."

So we invaded the block, roaming through the barracks, frightening naked children, catching young married couples unawares, drinking tea with old women. The Senator fondled babies, advised mothers, joked and shook hands with the men. I tried to explain the existence of a hot plate in Mrs. Yokata's room. "Senator, no food is allowed in the barracks. All meals are served in the dining halls. But . . ." He wasn't listening to me. He was staring at Mrs. Yokata. "Mother," he said, "what's on your mind? I'm here to listen to your problems."

"Senator Bone, she does not speak any English."

He became impatient with me. "What are you here for? Translate. Why does everybody want to leave me in the dark?"

Should I have told him that Mrs. Yokata's two oldest sons were in the Japanese Navy? That her husband was in an internment camp? That her youngest son, Tokuji, had run amok at Manzanar and tried to set fire to the barracks, and was now at the Moab isolation center in Utah?

"Senator, the supplies are short here, and Mrs. Yokata likes to suck on sugar occasionally."

"What's that?" he said. "Are they depriving her of sugar? WRA must be hoarding everything for itself."

I steered the Senator away from the bachelors' dorm, but he insisted on seeing the recreation hall. The radio was on at full blast, and Wendell Haraguchi was dancing with one of Mrs. Harada's daughters. He wore a zoot suit with zebra stripes for Senator Bone's visit. Mr. Haraguchi, I will have your nephew murdered one day, rest assured. And it will be soon. Wendell smiled when he saw me, fished a pair of fur earmuffs from his pocket, dangled them, and put them on in the middle of his dance; he spun his partner closer and closer to us. I drew the Senator into a conversation with two Kibei dentists who were discussing the general condition of evacuee teeth over their checkerboard. I left him there and approached Wendell. He bumped into me on purpose and then bowed profusely. "Excuse me, *Papa-san*."

I addressed his partner. "Miyo Harada, if your mother should discover the company you keep, she would raise a few welts on your back. And I will help her."

Miyo began to cry.

"Wendell, shut her up and get her out of here. I do not want trouble from you on this day. And if you have anything to say to me, first take off those earmuffs."

He comforted Miyo and then said, "Papa, my ears are cold."

"Wendell, you are clowning with the wrong person. The stove is on. It is roasting in here. Don't make a spectacle of yourself. Take off the earmuffs. I warn you. I know which goods you traffic in. I will have the police haul you in day and night."

"I'm clean, Papa. Always clean." He prompted Miyo, and she danced with him again, but she looked at the floor. "Papa, don't sleep too hard tonight. You might wake up with your throat cut." He laughed, stepped on my foot, removed the earmuffs, and flung them across the hall. The earmuffs sailed over the Senator's head, but he did not notice them. The Kibei dentists were examining his teeth. They followed us out of the recreation hall bearing their checkerboard. "Those shit-hole

Sacramento dentists," the Senator growled. I heard a hammer knock.

Nishitsujii the student, Harold's star reporter, was posting something on the bulletin board. Nishitsujii's broadsides are an outrage. But I usually have no trouble with him. As soon as he puts them up, Hiroshi takes them down. The dentists wanted me to confirm their diagnosis of the Senator's faulty bridgework; I excused myself and ran to the bulletin board. Nishitsujii's mouth was full of nails and thumbtacks. I looked over his shoulder. The poster was painted in clumsy, lopsided letters, Nishitsujii's inevitable trademark.

PATRIOTS OF BLOCK 38

THE STATE OF CALIFORNIA HAS ABANDONED US

IT HAS TAKEN OUR HOMES AND OUR FARMS

DO NOT CO-OPERATE WITH THIS HYPOCRITE

WHO COMES FROM THE LEGISLATURE

HE HAS MALIGNED YOU

HE HAS WISHED YOUR DEATHS

THE NISEI OF MANZANAR CAN HAVE NO

CHARITY FOR SUCH A MAN

HE DESERVES NOTHING

LET HIM TASTE THE DUST IN OUR MOUTHS

LET HIM LIVE WITH OUR FEARS

LET HIM SUFFER WITH US BEFORE HE COMES HERE

Gordon Y. Nishitsujii

I ripped the poster off the board and tore it up in front of him. "Student, Harold put you up to this. He thinks I have sabotaged his mimeograph machine, and this is his way of getting back. Tell your master that family relations mean nothing to Mitsuo. Brother-in-law or no brother-in-law, I will cripple him. He will put out his next issue from the stockade. I will hang him from the watertower. The coyotes will bay over his corpse. Do you hear?"

He spat the nails and thumbtacks into his palm. "Mitsuo," he said quietly, "Harold had nothing to do with it. This was my idea. You have outraged us, Mitsuo. You have sacrificed our dignity. You have compromised us."

I threw him off the porch.

"Nishitsujii, save your sentiments for another day. I will answer all your arguments. But not now. I am busy at the moment."

I ran back to the Senator. He insisted on taking the dentists with him on his travels through camp. My grimaces, my frowns, my black looks made no impression on them. They became the Senator's advisers. When I said, "Senator Bone, you will catch cold standing in the rain," they immediately took off their pea coats and draped them around the Senator. But they toppled their checkerboard at the same time, and while they pardoned themselves and stooped to pick up the checkers I led the Senator away from the recreation hall and left the dentists behind.

The Senator was incorrigible. He became involved

with a new party—Napoleon. Fumiko's tribe of brothers. Damn them all. Napoleon was walking hand in hand with Harold's featherbrained messenger boy, Spider Yoshima. The Senator saluted Napoleon and complimented him on his uniform. Napoleon was very proud. "I'm going to be a Navy pilot."

The Senator turned to me. "Mitsuo, who is this boy? We need more like him. Do you know him? Is he from this block?"

"Senator, he is my brother-in-law. Joseph is his real name. He calls himself Napoleon."

Spider Yoshima shuffled his feet nervously. He had never been near a Senator before. He did not know how to behave. Napoleon tugged the Senator's sleeve.

"Will you put Chuichi back in the Army, Senator, sir?"

I stepped between them and pulled Napoleon out of the way. "The Senator has nothing to do with the Army." I gave him a dime. "Go to the canteen. With Sam. If Fumi catches you walking in the rain she'll keep you inside for the rest of the week."

Napoleon took Sam's hand, and they trudged toward the canteen. The Senator huddled next to me.

"Mitsuo, take me to your quarters. I want to see where you live."

"Senator, I assure you, there is nothing special about my quarters. The barracks are all alike. No one receives preferential treatment here. My office is no bigger than a closet."

"Mitsuo, my feet are getting wet."

He will see the extra stove, the hot plate, the chocolate bars, the rows of canned goods, the ample supply of sugar; he will see that slut behind her paper curtain and think I am running a whorehouse or a home for unwed mothers; or perhaps he will think Ruby is my mistress. He will shout incest, perversion, rape, and I will be doomed. Beardsly will have no weapons to deal with the Senator's wrath. They will crucify me and send me to Moab to sit and rot.

Ruby wasn't behind her curtain. Chuichi was on his bed. He was wearing his Army shirt. He gave us both a silly, contemptuous grin. Someone must have fed him saké all morning. His breath was foul. The Senator ignored the canned goods and the chocolate bars; he stared at Chuichi's shirt.

"Soldier?" he said.

"My second brother-in-law. Chuichi. He was in the infantry."

"US infantry? Where were you stationed, soldier?" Chuichi continued to grin.

"Chuichi, the Senator is talking to you." He belched, spat into his boot, and turned his back on us. Fumiko came in. Her hands trembled. She hid them under her shawl.

"Fumi, find the Senator a pair of rubbers. Do you want him to catch cold?"

The rubbers didn't fit. The Senator sat on Chuichi's bed, and while he tugged and pulled, Fumiko helped him put them on. He was still wearing the dentists' two pea coats, and the extra sleeves flopped around him. I gave him an old hat to wear. We heard the sirens. The Senator jumped.

"It's lunchtime," I said.

I led the Senator to the door. A delegation was waiting for us. "Mitsuo, is that Beardsly and his damn crew? I won't eat with them. WRA is packed with Communists."

"Senator, it is only the council members of my own block. They are harmless, I assure you. They have nothing to do with the administration, and they are most anxious to meet you."

The councilmen lined up with their umbrellas in hand and bowed. I introduced them. "Yanaga, Barrack 3, Kobayashi, Barrack 11, Matsushita, Barrack 14 . . ." Mr. Yokata was holding the American flag. The Senator mingled with them immediately. The councilmen vied for the Senator's ear, and, huddling together, their umbrellas dipped and they poked one another accidentally with the spokes. I separated them and made them walk single file.

The Senator waved to children, made assurances to the councilmen, gave grandmothers and pregnant women the right of way; bands of evacuees began to swarm around him. A few Kibei spat when the Senator passed, but he paid no attention to them.

"Mitsuo," he called.

I was ten steps behind, and I had to walk around his admirers in order to get near him.

"Mitsuo, don't you see? If we throw out WRA we'll all be better off. The Army could train every man, woman, and child. Get everybody into shape. There wouldn't be any agitators. Nothing to agitate about. You're all good people. Mitsuo, what do you think?"

"Senator, I am not convinced that a military takeover would be in the best interests of the colony. You have been through the block. There was no trouble. Sen—"

He walked ahead, gripped the arms of two councilmen, and entered the mess hall. The other councilmen fell in behind him.

The Senator inspected the kitchen. He stirred the soup, tasted some peas, walked around the trays of mashed potatoes, stood near the oven, smelled the corned-beef hash; satisfied, he went to get his silverware. The councilmen wiped the moisture from his tray and made room for him at the front of the line. Toshio wasn't there. His number-three cook took charge and served the Senator heaping mounds of potatoes and hash.

When I arrived at his table the Senator was busy chatting with Ruby. She sat next to him and smiled maliciously at me. Slut, she never eats with us. Fumiko always brings lunch home for her. She chose this day to torment me. "My compliments, Mitsuo," the Senator mumbled. I thought he was talking about the food. "You have a very articulate sister-in-law." Is it possible that he did not notice her condition? Her belly was practically in his lap. "She says we ought to recruit the gals here. Make them rear-echelon soldiers. Free more of our boys to fight. Sensible girl."

Ruby hiccupped, and her belly rumbled.

Napoleon sat with Spider Yoshima at the other end of the table, helping him eat his soup. He made a bib with a paper napkin and two safety pins and fastened it to Spider's shirt. Harold was with Nishitsujii, staring at me, mocking me. The clatter of plates, the wailing of infants, the shrill laughter of the schoolgirls, the sour belches of the old men, the constant bustle, got on my nerves. I excused myself to the Senator, but he would not let me go. He gabbled at me. His mouth was full of food. "—miss my speech."

Councilman Matsushita poked me. "Mitsuo, the Senator cannot speak without an introduction. You must say something. Something very special. And then we will applaud."

I stood up. The citizens continued to lean over the tables, chatter, scratch themselves, and chew. The councilmen were enraged. They struck their cups relentlessly with spoons until the citizens looked up from their plates.

"Men and women of Block 38, as you all know, we

have with us today the distinguished Senator Gary Bone from Modoc County who has come to Manzanar to witness evacuee life. Senator Bone has long been a powerful force in the Legislature and has championed the rights of all the people of California." Harold frowned. Nishitsujii waggled his fingers behind his ears. I didn't care. "If we show the good Senator what our intentions are— that we are an honest people, that we are a patriotic people—I believe he will fight for us." Nishitsujii pretended to puke into his soup bowl. "Citizens, Senator Bone."

The citizens banged their plates, stamped their feet, whistled, shouted "Bone, Bone," and drowned out the few grumblers and catcallers. The Senator had not expected such enthusiasm at a Jap camp. The reception overwhelmed him for a moment. He cleared his throat, waited, and when the whistling and the banging began to die he raised his arms and asked for silence.

"Manzanites," he said. "Before coming to your colony, I was truly alarmed. Many of you must know that the Tule Lake relocation center is situated in my county. And it is because of the rioting and the sabotage at Tule Lake that I am forced to be here with you today. I am aware that you have relatives and friends at Tule Lake, and I can assure you that most of the colonists there are decent people like yourselves. But a small group of deceitful, evil men among the population is working hand in glove with the Fascist warlords. These men are paid servants and spies of the Japanese Government. They have taken over Tule Lake against the will of the majority and are using it as an enemy base, as an outpost for subversion and terror."

The grumblers began to multiply. The cooks retreated to the kitchen, the old bachelors made horrible faces and passed notes under the tables, and someone—it must have been Wendell—shouted, *"Shit on you and your spies!"* Councilman Matsushita climbed on the table and said, "Who speaks such filth in front of our honored visitor? Stand up, stand up. Show your ugly head." The zoot-suiters rose together; a little reluctant at first, a few of the bachelors joined them. The cooks wandered out of the kitchen. Harold and Nishitsujii stood up. Matsushita almost fell off the table. "Should we deport them all to Tule Lake, Senator Bone? Should we show them how lucky they are to be here?" The Senator asked Matsushita to come down, made conciliatory gestures to the zootsuiters and the others who were standing up, and sang a different song. He had perhaps exaggerated the conditions at Tule, he said. He was merely voicing the fears of many men and women in his county. He did not know of any specific cases of sabotage at Tule. And besides, his visit to Manzanar had dispelled many of his own fears. The zoot-suiters sat down. "I do not want to offend you," said Senator Bone. "I see decent, hard-working colonists around me." The councilmen beamed. Matsushita glared at me. I had failed to support the Senator during his moment of crisis. Slowly, expertly, the Senator relaxed and reassured the citizens. We were all great patriots, he said. "And I want you to know. I have the facts here. Assistant Camp Director Beardsly, your own Monroe Beardsly, has informed me that Manzanar is leading every other colony in the purchase of War Bonds and in the production and manufacture of coat linings and camouflage nets." A few of the citizens cheered. I stopped listening. The Senator's throat throbbed and swelled, and his lips puckered. I would have fallen asleep, but my councilmen gave me baleful looks. They will boycott my office in the future, I'm sure. They will complain to the Senator. They will conspire with Beardsly. Let Matsushita inherit my nineteen dollars a month together with all my other rights, privileges, and belongings. Let him deal with the complainers and the petitioners. Let him find a tub for the bachelors. Let him barter with the managers. Let him keep Toshio in line. Let him drill the Boy Scouts. I will take a holiday. I will stand near the gate and wave to the cars on the highway. I can still be of some service to the administration. I will give guided tours of the area. Senator, perhaps you will allow the Modoc County Parlor of the Daughters of the Golden West to visit us in a bunch? Don't worry. I will entertain them properly. Ladies—

Toshio arrived with his shock troops. Ten Kibei laborers from Block 11. Who let the bastards in? Toshio's cooks flocked around him. Chuichi was with them. The councilmen gave the Senator their undivided attention. They saw nothing. Two burly Jap policemen dozed near the entrance. The Senator growled and clawed the air. "—fight Fascism."

The cooks approached the Senator's table. Their hands were hidden. "—march together, fight together," the Senator said. "We will show—" A bruised banana bumped off his forehead before he could finish his sentence. Matsushita shrieked. The Jap policemen woke up and charged forward, shaking their billy clubs. The councilmen overcame their initial shock and put their bodies in front of the Senator. They were pelted with rotten fruit. "Good people," the Senator cried. "Please. Have you no shame?" The Kibei laborers disarmed the policemen. The bachelors were confused, embarrassed, and excited. They didn't join the melee; they urged the cooks on. The other citizens sat frozen in their seats. "Go back to Tule," one cook shouted and flung a blackened potato and an empty sugar box. Matsushita rallied the councilmen. He left the Senator's side for a minute, crouched, gathered up an armful of umbrellas while the garbage flew over his head, and gave them out to the councilmen. Holding the unfurled umbrellas before them like shields, the councilmen surrounded the Senator. "Go home," the cooks shouted together, and the citizens began picking up the chant.

The Senator reacted stoically to the garbage. He darted in front of the councilmen, ducking whenever necessary, appealed to the citizens, and tried to shame the cooks, but the shouting wrecked him. *Go home, go home, go home.* He withdrew into the cluster of umbrellas, remained there, and moaned. Matsushita dropped his umbrella. "Devils . . ." With the Senator no longer visible, the cooks aimed at Matsushita and me. They shot lima beans, split peas, banana skins, orange peels, and whatever else they could find. I was struck in the chest with a grimy spoon. I crawled under the table and met councilman Yanaga. "Mitsuo, what will become of us? The council tried to bring peace. We will be blamed for everything. Beardsly will say that we planned this affair for the Senator. He will take us into the wilderness and murder us. No one will know. Then he will find a new council." I stared at him. "Councilman Yanaga, control yourself. Beardsly can do nothing to us. We will not be blamed." The table moved, and our noses brushed. He apologized and backed away. I peeked out. Beardsly's marines had arrived. The bachelors collected their silverware and waited to be arrested. They were terrified, but they hoped the white policemen would search them and ask them questions and make their ordeal worth while. The cooks and the Kibei laborers picked up brooms and garbage-can lids and knelt behind an overturned table. The women gathered their children and ran toward the kitchen.

The policemen ignored the bachelors and the cooks. They pushed the councilmen aside, stepped over the garbage, and escorted the Senator out of the mess hall. The bachelors were keenly disappointed. When they discovered that Beardsly's marines were not going to arrest them they argued among themselves, and a fight broke out. My councilmen were useless. Numbed, confused, they milled about in their own little circle. I crawled out from under the table and scolded the bachelors. "Fools, what will you accomplish fighting among yourselves? Go back to your dormitory." The bachelors sulked and frowned. I seized a chair, stood on it, and shouted, "Hiroshi, where are you?" I had to shout again before he would stir. He climbed over the barricade. He was holding a broom. His face was dirty. His eyes were grim. His truculence startled me. I stepped down, shook him, and took away his broom. "Has Toshio converted you so soon? Help me clear the hall." I shook him again, and this time he complied. He became officious and barked orders in Japanese. I approached the blockade. "Citizens, we have some cleaning up to do." The cooks raised their garbage-can lids, peered at me, and grumbled; they wouldn't move.

I brought bewildered grandmothers back to their sons and daughters, I located lost children, I revived my councilmen and had them direct traffic for me. The women were afraid to come out of the kitchen. Hiroshi railed at them and threatened to lock them in. While he gestured, cursed, and scowled, Toshio gave up his barricade, pulled Hiroshi out of the way, spoke quietly to the women, escorted them out of the kitchen, and proved to them no white policemen were around. Wendell grinned at me and put on his earmuffs, but even the zootsuiters were cooperative. They lined up the bachelors and led them out. Still grumbling, the cooks picked up garbage and cleared the tables.

When Beardsly arrived with a riot gun and a full company of marines, there were only a few stragglers left in the mess hall. The policemen promptly chased them out. Beardsly was short with me. "Block manager Arimoto, I hold you personally responsible. I should arrest you, but I won't."

My councilmen would have fawned on him, they would have kissed his feet, but I wasn't in the mood. I sat down and smiled. *"Monroe, the whole thing was exaggerated."* I crossed my legs. He winced. He could not believe that I would take such liberties in front of his men. My Lord Beardsly, I have had a trying day. I am tired of rehearsing Boy Scout bands, I am tired of planning welcoming committees, I am tired of being an escort for Senators and fools. He saw that he would get no satisfaction from me, so he turned on his men. "Well, where's the riot?" He snatched the blunderbuss away from his sergeant-at-arms. "Do I see a riot?" The sergeant made a feeble attempt to answer. Beardsly shut him up. "The block manager claims we have exaggerated. He's right." Waving the blunderbuss, he dismissed his men. As soon as they left he straddled a chair, rocked back and forth awhile, and broke down. "Mitsuo," he blubbered, "I'm finished here. Kaput. Somebody's head will have to roll. And it won't be Swann's. Can't you people understand that it's all a question of equilibrium? You lean a little, we push a little. We have to keep up appearances. I don't care what you do in your barracks. But when somebody important comes, you have to toe the line."

He stood up, put on his pith helmet, wiped his eyes, and motioned to me. We walked out together. I carried the blunderbuss.

T*hree*

I have to wear two pairs of bloomers if I want to stay alive! The wind bites my belly button, and the ants want to sneak into my crack. The spiders are worse. You can't trust them after dark. God knows what's crawling in the dust! I'll scream if I have to sit here another minute. Why can't anything work out right? *You* order a brassiere from a catalogue! Montgomery Ward thinks pregnant girls grow udders. I'll have to wait until I'm a granny before I can wear it. My nipples hurt. Where's Wendell? Chuichi came in and I stuck my face into the curtain and watched him undress. His calves are round and hard, and he's so strong he has muscles in his behind! If Wendell doesn't come soon I'm going to be in trouble. I'll make a deal with Napoleon. I'll give him a quarter (a real quarter, not one of Wendell's slugs) if he'll let me sneak into his bed and stay with Chuichi the whole night. I just want to watch the way Chuichi sleeps.

Napoleon wouldn't let me. I'd have to strangle him first. What if I walked up to Chuichi while he was sleeping and whispered in his ear, *Chuichi, stay with me*. I won't tell a soul. We can dance and my belly won't get in the way. I'll close the curtain. Who cares if it's a sin! What else do I have to do? I can't even walk out of my room. The neighbors hiss, and the bachelors say dirty things. I could make four dollars, four dollars a day (more than Mitsuo makes, more than Wendell makes), and all I would have to do is touch them. Who wants to? The bachelors have diseases.

He threw his shoes in first, because he can never climb through the window wearing them; then I saw his arm shoot over the sill, and it dangled the way it always does, and he said, "Help me, I'm loaded down." So I pulled him in. He sat on the floor and started to laugh. "Oh what's that, what's that?"

I hit him over the head with my jewelry box, hard, because I meant it. "It's a nursing bra, you jackass. Don't you know anything about people?"

"A nursing bra?" He was curious as hell, and he wanted me to put it on.

"Oh Wendell, you are the stupidest person around. The bra is for the baby, so you can feed him." I showed him how the cups open, and he had a laughing fit right on the floor. I reached for the jewelry box and he stopped.

He picked up the bra and poked his hands through the holes.

"Groovy," he said.

I hit him again, harder.

"Wendell Haraguchi, don't you talk like a nigger in front of me. You know I can't stand it when you talk like a nigger."

He felt his head, frowned at me, and said, "You made me a bump."

"I'll give you another if you don't behave."

He jumped up. "I'm going home. I didn't come here for bumps."

I grabbed his coattails and gave them a pull. I heard something rip.

"You crazy?" he said. "Where am I gonna find a tailor at midnight?"

I gave the tails another pull. "What did you bring me, Wendell?"

"Nothing."

I put my hands inside his coat and tickled his ribs. He started to howl. "Big Papa wakes up, he'll bring in the MPs. And what do you think they'll do if they catch me here after curfew?"

We sat on my bed and Wendell emptied his pockets and put everything in my lap. He brought me a compact with pearls in it, five chocolate cordials wrapped in silver (I'll bet they were stale because you can't get any silver foil now, so they must have been wrapped before the war) a Mother Hubbard sewing set, a jar of honey, a book about Indians, and a contraption that had a nozzle with a bulb and a bottle attached to it.

"That's the seventh compact you brought me so far, Wendell."

Wendell exploded. "You want variety during wartime? Things are tight, very tight, especially with the Army recruiters around. I risk my neck every night . . ."

He caught me looking at the contraption, and he smiled.

"Don't you smile at me." I shook the bottle and squeezed the bulb. "I know what it is. It's for warming the baby's milk."

"You telling me what it's for? I took it from the commissary. That's an atomizer. Opera stars use it. When they have a sort throat. You put perfume in, and you squeeze."

"Opera stars," I said. "Only an idiot would ever spray his throat with perfume." But Wendell wasn't listening. So I shook him.

"Take me dancing."

He didn't like the idea. "You aint supposed to dance before you have a baby. You want it to be born a freak?"

"That isn't why you won't take me. You're ashamed. You don't want anybody to see you with me. You want to dance with the high-school girls. So you can win the marathon when the Bombers come."

"Somebody's been telling you stories. How are the Bombers supposed to get to California? Most of them are in Gila."

"Mr. Swann is going to bring them here for Washington's Birthday. They're going to play at all the centers. And at the Army bases."

"Shit, I don't want nothing to do with no band that plays at an Army base."

"We don't have to go to the marathon, Wendell. We can dance right here."

"You want to wake up the whole camp? You're crazy."

I sat on him and pulled his ears. "You'd be crazy too if you had to stay in one room all day."

"Don't I bring you the movie magazines from the canteen?"

"I'm sick of movie magazines. Would *Screenland* tell you if Shirley Temple missed her period? Did Gary Cooper ever come to Manzanar?"

"So why don't you go outside? Beardsly isn't after you. He's after me."

"I can't."

"Has anybody been making fun of you?" Wendell said, and he was mad. He got up and strutted around, only there wasn't enough room for him, and he tripped against my lamp. He would have crashed through the curtain and landed in Mitsuo's lamp, but I caught him in time. "I catch anybody making fun of you, you know what will happen." He took out his switchblade. "I don't care if it's a kid or somebody's gramma. No mercy. Why can't you go outside?"

"Because the bachelors bother me. That's why. They say nasty things when they see me walking."

His blade was open even before I heard the click. "Was it Uncle?"

"Oh Wendell, what would your uncle want with me? He's too old."

"Who was it then?"

"I can't remember their names."

He grabbed my hand. "Come on. I'm taking you to the dorm. I don't care about curfew. Just point them out to me when we get there. I'll hang them upside down and let their brains leak out."

"It isn't only the bachelors who bother me. You know the guard in the tower near the factory, the one you always deal with."

"Goodyear?" Wendell said. "What about him?"

"Well, Marsha Yamaji says he's been talking about me."

"How the hell does Marsha know? She been up to the tower?"

"No! She works in the factory. She sees him after lunch."

"I'll bet," Wendell said. "I'll bet he gives her a bang in the tower every night."

"You better not say that, Wendell. Marsha's my

friend. She wouldn't fool around with a guard. She hates soldiers."

Wendell smirked and picked his nails. "What did Goodyear say?"

"He has a name for me."

"What name?"

"It's dirty. It starts with a c."

"Mother, what's the name?"

"*Cuntie pie.*"

His coattails went flying, and he would have been out the window if I didn't grab his leg and hold on. "I'll roast him in his frigging tower."

"Wendell, maybe Marsha made it up. Maybe she meant a different guard." I tickled him, I squeezed his ribs, but he kept right on climbing. "Wendell it couldn't have been Goodyear. I never met him. Wendell—why did you bring me a book about Indians?"

He stopped climbing.

"Indians are important."

"Who told you that? All they do is live in a reservation."

He sat down and crossed his legs. "Who put them there? Who took away their rights? You think Manzanar isn't a reservation? That's why we have to study about the Indians. Tosh knows. We're going to end up the same way."

"What way?"

"Fratricide," he said, and he stuck out his lips.

I looked at him, because when Wendell makes a face something is on his mind. "Are you a Communist, Wendell? How come you use words that nobody can understand?"

"It's simple." He dropped his chin between his knees. "The government is going to put the Indians and the Hindus in with us, and maybe the niggers, and we're never going to get out of camp alive. We're going to be wiped out."

"Stop scaring me, Wendell. Mitsuo wouldn't work for Mr. Swann if we were all going to get killed." I didn't believe him, but I caught the hiccups and I started to cry.

Wendell moved closer. "What are you crying for? You think I'm going to let anything happen to you? We're safe for now. But when they start bringing in the Hindus, we'll know what to do."

"Stop it, Wendell. You know what happens when you scare me. I have to pee."

"You pee all the time."

"Well, you're supposed to pee a lot when you're pregnant." I made him turn around. I took out the paint can Mitsuo gave me, pulled down my drawers, and peed. Wendell laughed at the sound it made. "Don't you snigger, Wendell Haraguchi. I didn't ask you to come. You can just walk out the same way you arrived if you keep that up. You didn't see me climbing through any windows." He didn't say anything. I frowned and put the can away. "Tell me about the recruiting team, Wendell. Are the Army men making everybody sign up?"

"No Army man is gonna make me register." He started strutting again. "Anybody from this block who registers gets his throat cut. Uncle gave the word. It's automatic."

"Oh bother! I'll bet your uncle thinks he's Fu Manchu. He can't even control the bachelors. Stay away from him, Wendell. He has bad ideas."

"Change the subject," Wendell said, and I could feel the meanness blowing through him.

"Don't be stubborn, Wendell. You better give up your habits. You're going to be a father in less than sixty days."

"Change the subject, y'hear?"

When Wendell gets sullen, it takes hold of him like a dust devil; his face turns black, his eyes bulge, his body shakes, and you have to wait until it passes over him. I didn't want to say something important because Wendell can't listen too hard when he gets this way, so I started talking about Fumi. "Sis is just like Mom. They wouldn't leave Dad in peace. He had to run to the bars. Yabos aren't too popular in Watsonville. Dad got into fights when he was drunk, and Chuichi rescued him. Mom and Sis ganged up on him later, and Dad had to sleep on the porch with the dogs. Wendell, do you believe in ghosts? Fumi says our ancestors will haunt us if they find out about my condition. She makes my life miserable!"

"Yak, yak, yak," Wendell said, and he was laughing, so I knew he was all right. "You yak about your sister and you yak about your Dad. Shit, man."

Wendell expected me to shout at him because of his nigger talk, but I didn't. I wasn't going to give him the opportunity to be sullen again. So I said, "Wendell, say the dirtiest thing you know. I don't care."

Wendell was suspicious.

"I can't. It's too dirty." So he wrote it on a piece of paper with the pencil stub he always carries in his coat. He folded it up and gave it to me. I didn't know what to expect. I unfolded it and put it near the light bulb. All it said was UNCLE SAM. "Oh Wendell." I hugged him and I tickled him. I felt his arms and his chest under his coat, and I don't know what happened, but I got on top of him.

"What you want?" he said.

"Fuck me, Wendell, please. Or put your finger in."

He got up. "You crazy! This is a social call. You think people are deaf? Didn't the doctor tell you? It aint good for the baby."

"I get lonely sometimes, Wendell."

"Don't I come here every night? Don't I bring you presents? Swann catches me with stolen goods he won't bother with any jail. He'll put me in the penitentiary."

"Who asks you to come if it's such a sacrifice." I was so mad I started to shout. "You never complained when you took me to the storage room or by the grandstand.

— *66* —

You begged me to come. I had to bribe Napoleon so I could sneak out." The curtain stirred. "Damn you," Wendell said, and he jumped out the window. "Damn you, Ruby, damn you." His butt was halfway over the sill, but he changed his mind, came back, kissed me, squeezed my tit, and took the nursing bra for a souvenir. I tossed out his shoes. And I hid the compact and the cordials just in time. Fumi came through the curtain. First I thought she was walking in her sleep because her eyes were closed and she stumbled around, but then I saw the look on her face. She was furious. "Where's your baby gangster?" she said.

"There isn't anybody here! You want to search under the bed?"

She put out the light. I don't like being with Fumi in the dark. You can't tell if she's going to hug you or pull your hair. So I curled up and pulled the blanket over my head. I waited until I heard her bed creak, then I threw off the blanket and went over to the window. Wendell was at the end of the block. He was running with his back hunched so the guards wouldn't see him. His long coat scraped the ground.

Four

IN THE COLONY

with Hal Tanaka

Our Administration has invited the *Patriot* to help
publicize the combined War Department and WRA
drive to register all adult evacuees. The registration,
claims Project Director S., is the first step in restoring
full civil liberties to us. What are we to believe? Captain
J. O. Prudhomme and his Army registration team are at
Manzanar to process our young men for voluntary in-
duction in the all-Nisei combat unit which "will prove
once and for all the fighting spirit of Americans with
Japanese blood." What are we to believe? Mr. S. tells us
that the new policy of WRA is to vigorously support our
requests for indefinite leave, in the hope of eventually
resettling the entire Manzanar population. Yet in the
past anyone who has asked for leave clearance has been
given the runaround by Washington and been harassed
by the FBI. Who are we to believe? The questionnaires

of the Army and WRA turn out to be loyalty oaths in disguise. Citizens and aliens alike are asked to pledge allegiance to America, to forswear allegiance to Japan, and our young men are asked to state their willingness to serve in the armed forces.

Those of us who have answered "No-No" to the loyalty questions have indicated to America that it has lost its right to ask allegiance of us. The "No-Noes" have been threatened by the Army. Captain Prudhomme has appeared at our mess halls to notify us that if we interfere with his registration we "can look forward to a $10,000 fine and twenty years in jail." We tried to join his Army once, and we were refused. And many of our brothers and cousins who were in the Army before the war were kicked out. Now the good Captain would like us to volunteer for his segregated suicide squad. How many other American soldiers were inducted from behind barbed wire?

Jack of diamonds, queen of spades, redeem your deeces, save your kings. Swann has retired me from active duty. He's shut down the *Patriot* while the Army recruiters are at camp, and Gordon has taught me pinochle in the interim. We play every day. Paper is scarce, and I tally the scores on the walls. Gordon is thousands of points ahead. He learned the game from an old Jew who owned a fruit stand in Anaheim. Gordon worked for him after studying botany and American literature at UCLA for seven years. Pinochle is a very wicked game. I can't keep track of all my aces and kings, I forget to meld marriages, and Gordon has learned to husband his trump cards: he wins every trick in the play-offs.

"Gordon, I'll scream if we play another hand."

He shuffled the cards.

"I'm serious. Euchre, hearts, California Jack, but no pinochle. It's a disease."

He dealt me double ace and double ten of trump. The aces made me delirious. I put on my pea coat, but I thrust my arm through the wrong sleeve, and Gordon had to untangle me. I ran out of the office.

"Hal, wait."

We ran across the firebreaks, behind the factories and the warehouses, in front of the hospital, between the barracks, and after startling Myrna, the pregnant goat in Block 32's children's zoo, stalling a brigade of washer-women who clucked at us as the dust rose, and breaking through a squad of security police who laughed and yawned because they knew we were harmless and had nothing better to do, Gordon caught up with me near the post office. We had to rest on the steps before we could say a word.

"It's hopeless. Come on."

We went back to the office.

The Yes-Yeses and the No-Noes are at war. The Yes-Yeses shout "Fascist pig," and the No-Noes scream back *aka*—red—and *inu*—dog. The Yes-Yeses are led by the former chiefs of the Japanese-American Citizens League, who are now block managers and members of the Manzanar Community Council. The No-Noes are more amorphous. The block managers call them warmongers and stooges of the Emperor and claim that their leaders at camp are Professor Ifukube, old man Haraguchi, and the Kibei cooks. But if you ask Kayama, the head of the Community Council, he will tell you: *These men are part of a network of spies and fifth columnists that is trying to seize control of the relocation program. They take their orders from Tokyo.* Secret societies have sprung up in support of the No-Noes. The most notorious of them, the Blood Brothers Corps, has threatened to kill Kayama, "Public Inu No. 1," for being a tool of the administration and a paid informer for the FBI. So far they have limited their activities to slashing the tires of Captain Prudhomme's jeep.

Mitsuo is dreadfully afraid of the Blood Brothers. He interrupted my dart game at the canteen today and took me aside. "Harold, block manager Murakami woke up this morning with an x painted in blood on his forehead. No one is safe. They will cut out his tongue if he speaks up at the council meeting. Do something."

"Mitsuo, I have no immunity. The Brothers threaten everybody. I wouldn't be surprised if I woke up with an x myself."

His eyes closed. He was terrified. "Harold, do not say

such a thing. It will bring us bad luck. If the Brothers come after you, do you think they will leave me unmarked? But they like you. You denounced Swann's administration in print. Harold, you must prepare a special bulletin for the Brothers. Tell them that the block managers are their friends. We are all working for—"

I walked away. He pushed me and shouted, but the dart players stared at him, and he calmed down. He did not want the people in his own block to talk about him. He smiled, joked with the dart players, blew his nose, and bought a candy bar. The commotion ruined my game. I aimed without conviction, and the darts struck the outer circles of the board.

Gordon and I have been deposed. Before Swann shut us down, all the factions at camp came to us for information. They could not afford to get on our bad side. We knew Manzanar inside out, and the wheelers and dealers dreaded our exposés. We were not self-righteous. We didn't bother the managers when they bargained among themselves for supplies, we said nothing when the cooks snatched a little food from the warehouse for their friends, but when the warehouse crews cut back the rations of each block so they could create a scarcity and force the canteens to charge exorbitant prices, we had them thrown out. And when the gamblers of Block 11 tried to establish a prostitution ring by threatening and cajoling two fifteen-year-old girls, Gordon devoted one sentence to them in his weekly column, "Views from the Hangman's Corner," and the gamblers had to beg Swann to send them to another camp.

Now we're out of touch. Swann no longer sends his couriers to us. Beardsly ignores us. His guards make fun of us. The block managers call us Fascists; the secret societies say we're Communists and collaborators. I'm afraid the warehousemen have begun hoarding food again, and pretty soon there'll be a run on candy bars at the canteen. Worst of all, our sources of information have disappeared. Even if we scoured the camp ourselves we would find out nothing. The news escapes us. We can hardly keep up with the activities of our block. Gordon has the shivers every morning. It pains him to be so cut off. Not even his fabulous scores in pinochle help. I tried to drag him over to Swann's office. "Gordon, I insist. Tell Swann that you disassociate yourself utterly and completely from my editorial policies, and he'll put you in charge of the *Patriot*. Don't worry about me. I'll write articles for you on the sly."

He refused.

Sometimes we do stumble onto things. We happened to be in the latrine when the No-Noes were organizing a rally. They didn't monkey around. When the men standing outside failed to respond fast enough to their invitations, the organizers whacked their shins with sticks and herded them into the latrine. We were pushed against the wall. Gordon smiled. "It must be the professor. He enjoys rough tactics." In a few minutes Professor Ifukube's Kibei bodyguards arrived. They slammed us with their chests and made a path for the professor. He was wearing a black cloak and high boots. Togo Ifukube is a bitter, spiteful little man with ice in his veins and bile in his heart. He was my counselor at Stanford for five years. He taught anatomy and was the honorary head of the Japanese Students' Association. He lived with us at the student clubhouse. He spied on us, he went through our belongings, he made the other students wait on him and wash his shirts, he damned us if we came in late or received poor grades, he called us devils if we brought a white woman to the clubhouse. Professor Ifukube had no trouble with English before he came to camp. Now he speaks only Japanese.

Gordon nudged me. The professor must have shouted something. The organizers saluted him and made us bow. "We're in for it," I said. Ifukube began to rave. His face swelled, his eyes rolled in his head, his body shook beneath his cloak. He shouted some gibberish about the old order and the new, about Japan's destiny and America's imminent collapse. He recited a Japanese proverb about an octopus and a crab, but I couldn't catch the meaning. Gordon and I wanted to leave. We didn't dare. The professor's Kibei bodyguards were sumo champions, and they would have broken our necks. One of them stared at me. I decided to pay more attention to the professor's speech. He condemned to death anyone who cooperated with the Army or the administration. Then he became incoherent. He mumbled, he snarled. Something must have irked him, because he grabbed a stick from an organizer and attacked his bodyguards. Cowering and yelping, they begged him not to flay them. Gordon was appalled, but I was familiar with the professor's behavior. He turned around, screamed, and beat anyone within range. It's obvious," Gordon said. "His target is the whole world." We all fled, pushing and tripping over one another as we crowded through the door. I heard someone scream behind me. Ifukube was still swinging.

My two secretaries, Miss Akira and Miss Tokutomi, have come around to the office looking for things to do. They won't go to work for Swann. Their loyalty touches me. I'm ashamed to say I've laid them both. At Manzanar the usual taboos on relations between employers and employees have no meaning. I may have been their boss, yes, but we're all in the same boat. Still, I should have been less selfish about my pleasures. Now that they are no longer virgins, Miss Akita and Miss Tokutomi will have a hard time finding husbands for themselves.

Gordon had a fit when he saw me giving dictation to

the girls. His scowls were so severe I had to send them home.

"Storing up articles for the future, Harold? Or are you planning to take the *Patriot* underground?"

"It has nothing to do with the paper," I said. "I'm writing my memoirs."

He threw a piece of wood at me.

"Why should you complain if I keep them busy?"

"Harold, let them find another occupation. Yoko"—Miss Akira—"can sew. Chieko"—Miss Tokutomi—"can operate a kiln. Don't encourage them to come here."

Gordon won't admit it, but he's fond of Yoko. He's had a thousand opportunities to seduce her, but he hasn't taken advantage of any of them. Gordon is the wonder virgin of Manzanar. His columns, his articles, his poems, his anagrams, his riddles, and his editorial cartoons were once the favorite reading of every factory girl, seamstress, and schoolteacher at camp. They flocked to the office, they wanted private lessons, they begged him to explain his riddles, and Gordon chased them away. I offered to divert them to my corner of the office. Gordon would have none of it. He warned them. "My commander-in-chief is a bandy-legged satyr. He suffers from acute myopia and an unknown liver ailment. He's poison. Stay away." Gordon's purity gives me headaches. He says he will never touch a girl unless he marries her first, and he cannot get married in such evil times, so he will have to abstain until after the war. I try to put holes in his logic. "Fool. Who knows when the war will end? Be a glutton for once in your life. Flesh spoils."

It does no good. All I get for my efforts is a frown, and if I persist, a slap.

Prudhomme lives in his jeep. Sergeant Milton Erasmus Sato, his chauffeur, interpreter, and aide-de-camp, drives him around while Prudhomme sits up on the boot of the jeep with his visor down and salutes everybody in sight. He thinks this is a good way of advertising himself and his cause. Sergeant Sato is a reckless driver, and someday he will run over one of the old men who stroll in front of the jeep, but the children love him because he beeps at them. Sergeant Sato was only a private before the war. No one knows why he has prospered when most of the other Nisei soldiers were discharged after Pearl Harbor.

Swann's aides have been in and out of my office. They crawl along the floor taking measurements, they look slyly at our pinochle scores on the wall, and they make believe we aren't there. We sing songs to them, we compose obscenities about the Army, we continue to mark up the walls, but they still ignore us. Perhaps Swann has had some second thoughts about closing down the *Patriot*. Prudhomme must have put the pressure on him. The campaign to recruit men for the Nisei combat unit has been a total flop. Sato has visited every block, but if Mitsuo is right, only a handful of men have volunteered.

Prudhomme is hungry for publicity, but Swann wants no part of me. I'm sure he's been shopping for a new editor.

The new editor shows up. It's Daniel L. Hayashi, camp historian. He tells us that we have another day to move out our things. Swann is not taking any chances. Daniel L. Hayashi is pro-American, pro-Prudhomme, and pro-Swann. For the past few months Danny and his staff have been in the field taking surveys for WRA. Swann has commissioned him to prepare a history of Manzanar for future generations. I would like to take a peek at Danny's history. I know he won't slander us or resort to lies. His corps of photographers won't pass over the tar-paper barracks or the watchtowers and the shithouses, but Danny's captions will claim that our hardships are helping to win the war. He will label us the new pioneers. He won't forget the scrap-metal collections and the War Bond drives at camp; he'll show evacuee carpenters installing fireboard ceilings in the barracks, construction crews building roads, evacuee firemen on the job; he'll interview Issei bachelors who broke their backs for thirty years working in labor gangs up and down the coast and are now on a "holiday" at Manzanar; he'll talk about the Americanization of grandmothers and Nisei housewives in Swann's adult-education program; he'll even record the gripes of individual evacuees. But will he talk about the hostility, the shame, the inadequacy, the confusion that we all, even Danny Hayashi, share to some degree? Will he say that it makes no difference whether we praise the Emperor or bless Swann's administration, that we have been betrayed, tricked, ignored, and abandoned by both countries?

Danny has not disappointed us. The first issue of the new *Patriot* is an homage to Prudhomme. Page one is devoted to the Army recruiting program and the one and only Nisei combat unit. There's a lengthy exchange between Swann and Prudhomme about what we can expect after we win the war. There's a feature article by Danny himself about Sergeant Sato's spiraling career in the Army. And, as an added attraction, there's a comic strip entitled "The Conversion of Joe Watanabe, from Wastrel and Teen-Age Profligate to All-American Nisei, Who Brings Honor to His Country and His People by Joining the 442nd Regimental Combat Team." Gordon was outraged. "Let Swann and Prudhomme play with each other on the front page, let Sato tell his success story, I can live with that, but does Danny Hayashi have to use comics to peddle his shit?"

We waited until after dark to take our revenge. We stole into the office and prepared our own comic strip on Danny's stencils. Gordon worked on the drawings, I did the balloons. Our hero was a combination daredevil and samurai warrior. He wore a mask, a cape, and two swords. He was a pervert, an acrobat, and a thief. We called him the Nippon Pimpernel. He picked his nose in the first panel. He held up the commissary in the second, joined an extortion ring in the third. Later on he exposed the ring and turned out to be an undercover agent for WRA. Throughout the action he kept one hand suspiciously in his front pocket.

We ran off the comic strip on the mimeo machine, put copies on the bulletin boards, stuffed them in block managers' mailboxes, taped them to the walls of the latrines, and left a stack in Prudhomme's jeep.

Blackstone, Swann's information officer, had us hauled in. Swann picked the right man to intimidate us. There is nothing foreboding about Blackstone. He's neither short nor tall; he doesn't leer, he doesn't shout; he won't twist your arm or shame you with a wink or a kiss; but he's still the terror of the camp. Gordon thinks he's a master of psychological torture; I'm not so sure. There's just no way of avoiding him. Blackstone gave us a break. He left us with Lovelady, his assistant. We sat in the administration building, between two special policemen, while Lovelady grilled us. "Cocksuckers," he said. "You miserable, spineless little cocksuckers." The special policemen were delighted with Lovelady's tactics. Gordon and I were bored. I prayed that Blackstone would stay away.

Lovelady produced the comic strip. He put it rudely in front of Gordon's nose. "See this, cowboy? It's treason, pure and simple." He leaned over us. "Nippon Pimpernel, ay?" He was debating whether to bang our heads together. I wouldn't have complained. A good knock on the head might have put my mind to rest. Lovelady must have been working overtime. He had prepared a confession for us during his off hours. He accused us of wanting to incite a riot, of undermining evacuee morale, of engaging in pornography and other treasonable activities, of daring to question the intentions of WRA and the authority of the United States Army, of being Bolsheviks, Blood Brothers, and queers. We refused to sign.

"Frame-up," Gordon said.

I agreed. "I'll tell Swann."

"Blackstone will break his ass."

I knew what was coming next. We were taking Lovelady's confession a little too lightly. The special policemen laughed. Gordon's head must be harder than mine. I didn't see any stars, but my ears rang and my eyes leaked.

"You can't kid me," Lovelady said. "You think I'm stupid?" We didn't know what to say. "You expect me to believe that the grass and the sky changed places overnight? Nobody could have done those drawings except Nishitsujii. Admit it. And you," he said, pointing his finger at me. "You're the mastermind. You put him up to it. The student doesn't make a move without you." He was putting on a show for the policemen. He grabbed my collar. "You know how many times this little cocksucker riled me? And I couldn't touch him. Why? Because there was a hands-off policy before Swann dumped him. He was top man in the colony with his miserable newspaper, which I wouldn't waste my time reading because it's Jap junk, that's all. But now . . ."

Blackstone came in.

"Chief," Lovelady said, "give me two more minutes and I'll have them signed, sealed, and delivered."

Blackstone noticed my rumpled collar and the bump on my head. Lovelady disappeared with his two policemen.

"I'm sorry," Blackstone said. "I shouldn't have had you come when Emmett was here. He gets carried away."

He picked up the comic book. Gordon was stiff and kept a poker face, but I began to shake.

"I confess," I said. "We did it. It was our job. Lock us up."

"Hal, Hal," Blackstone said, and he laughed.

"It's true. It was childish, I admit. But Lovelady's all wet. Treason wasn't on my mind. Danny Hayashi's edition was an insult. We had to pay him back."

Gordon gave me no support. He slumped in his chair and scowled.

Blackstone let us go.

Gordon abused me on the way back to our block.

"Blackstone shit in your face and you never even knew

it. He had no intention of locking us up. Do you think Emmett's roughhousing was an accident? Blackstone had it timed. He came in at the right moment so he could play the beneficent father. And you swallowed it."

"Stop shoving me, Gordon. Talk but don't shove."

We wrestled on the firebreak. I pinned his arms and shouted in his face. "What can I do? Blackstone has a power over me. I'm helpless."

I released him, and when I tried to get up Gordon bit me on the ass.

I warned him. "This is war."

Danny Hayashi's issues keep coming, each one a little worse than the other. Prudhomme is still the center of attraction, and in spite of the secret societies the recruiting has picked up. We've grown immune to Joe Watanabe, All-American Nisei, who is currently on maneuvers in Mississippi with the 442nd. As soon as Danny is finished for the day Gordon and I move in. But Swann has wised up. He's installed a guard outside the office every night, and now we have no place to congregate, and Gordon has no place to sleep. He intends to live with the bachelors.

Our habits haven't changed much. Pinochle and darts at the canteen, volleyball in the gym, but without the office to comfort us we've been getting on each other's nerves. It's nobody's fault; even our battles seem forced. We're trying a temporary separation. It wasn't planned.

We just avoid each other. I began hanging out in Mitsuo's office, but it's being used these days to register the block for Swann and the Army; the registrars monopolize the area around the stove, and I can't even keep my hands warm. So I stay home.

It doesn't pay to get out of bed. Napoleon brings me candy bars, and I spend my time observing Fumiko's sovereignty over our one room. She assigns us cupboard space, she regulates the volume of Ruby's record player, she moves our beds around. Nothing can take place here without her consent. Mitsuo isn't allowed to bring his politics home, Napoleon can't have his pet lizards and snakes, and I'm not allowed to drink beer or smoke.

The registration has given us a temporary reprieve. Fumiko is in Mitsuo's office today, helping the old Issei men fill out the WRA questionnaires. Napoleon runs for Spider Sam. They come back with lizards, snakes, cigars, and cigarettes, and, with Fumiko gone, I hold court on my bed. We play with the lizards, we smoke, we spill some beer. On impulse I say, "Poleon, find Gordon. Bring him to the party. Tell him, let's have a truce." Napoleon runs out again. I sit with Spider Sam.

"Ruby."

She peeks through her curtain.

"Put on Tommy Dorsey. Me and Sam want to dance."

Sam is shy, and he holds me loosely while we jitterbug. Ruby turns up the volume. I spin Sam around and show

— 85 —

him a new step, but his heart isn't in it. His body is tense, his moves are awkward. He slips, I catch him, and instead of dancing we begin to spar. He circles around me, smiling, hopping. Ignoring the phonograph, he dances to the rhythms in his head. He blocks my first punch, ducks under the second, snorts, ties me up, taps me gently, and socks me on the jaw.

Napoleon comes in. He doesn't seem surprised to see me sitting on the floor. I raise my head and look for Gordon. "He wouldn't come?"

Napoleon shakes his head.

"Why should he?" I say. "It's time we both saw some new faces. Come on, we'll have our party without him."

Sam stoops to help me up, but his expression changes; he pulls back, stiffens, and hops around the room with a pained look on his face. Ruby runs behind her curtain. Napoleon hides behind me. The apocalypse is upon us. Fumiko is wielding her broom. She swats Spider Sam. "Take advantage of me," she says. She curses Sam's ancestors. She's about to deliver a haymaker, but her attention is diverted for a moment. She sees the lizards and the snakes. She shrieks. I make a grab for the broom. I'm rewarded with blows on either shoulder. I do a somersault for her. "You are the guilty one," she says. She's very formal with me. *"Oniisan,* do you think you can have a circus the minute I am gone? Good-for-nothing. With your prizefighter bum for a companion. Do you want to corrupt the children?" The broom misses me by an inch. I feint once, dart in and out, and while Fumi is busy with Napoleon I take away her broom.

Sam Yoshima was born on Queen Emma Street in the heart of Honolulu's Japtown. He would have stayed home for the rest of his life, but there happened to be a shortage of Japanese boxers on the mainland ten years ago. An Oakland promoter discovered him in a Queen Emma Street pool hall. Sam was over thirty. He had been a ditchdigger for years, his teeth were bad, he couldn't spell and he could barely count; he had no admirers and few friends. The promoter didn't care. He wanted Sam for the tank towns. He needed someone who could take a steady drubbing without complaints. He collected ten yabos like Sam, gave each of them a freshly minted hundred-dollar bill, and brought them to America. The other yabos were a little smarter and luckier than Sam. They got their heads broken the requisite number of times and returned to Queen Emma Street in two years. But Sam was persistent. He couldn't believe that anyone would pay him just to see him get beaten up. When he decked the home-town hero in Sebastopol the crowd threw bottles at him. When he did it again in Castroville the local gamblers knocked him senseless after the fight. The Oakland promoter began to take notice. He gave him Spider for a nickname, added him to his permanent stable, and allowed him to graduate from the preliminary bouts to the quarter-finals.

Spider made ten dollars more every week, but he was hit twice as hard and much more often. Still, he was making a name for himself. Sam had taken an unconscionably long time to bloom, and the promoter, sensing that his clientele would quickly lose interest in a thirty-five-year-old fighter with bad teeth, promptly chopped ten years off Sam's age and billed him as the new Jap bantam wonder. It worked for a while. Issei and Nisei in every Japtown from San Diego to Seattle flocked to see Sam fight. Sam lost half his teeth to Homicide Hank Shimazu at Dreamland Auditorium in San Francisco, Kid Manila closed both his eyes at Hollywood Legion Stadium, but whenever Sam fell apart, the promoter stuck his magic key in Sam's ass, wound him up, and dispatched him to Gilroy or Yuba City for his next fight. Sam broke down permanently in Eureka. The magic key was inserted, but Sam's mainspring was shot. So the promoter gave him another freshly minted hundred-dollar bill and left him in Eureka.

The evacuation saved Sam.

He doesn't have to worry about crossing streets, he won't get picked up for vagrancy, and he has Napoleon to remind him to eat. Gordon and I ran a feature on Sam last October. We should have protected his anonymity, but we were tired of praising WRA and were hungry for news. At first the bachelors wouldn't leave him alone. They put pennies in his pockets and made him show his muscles and tell stories. The children took advantage of his goodness, tricked him, and stole his pennies. There's been a lull lately. The children are tired of him, the bachelors are preoccupied with the registration, and Sam's been forgotten again.

Mitsuo is disturbing the equanimity of my life in bed. The Blood Brothers have included him on their latest death list, and he's decided to sit home. He has delusions about my position vis-à-vis Swann and insists I have enough pull to get a military policeman installed in our room. Denials, horse laughs, farts, appeals to logic have no effect. He takes hold of my pajamas. "It's up to you, Harold. You can save me." Since I can't come up with anything, I have to suffer the consequences. He's made me his sentry. I sit near the window and report to him any face, foreign or familiar, within a hundred feet. Mitsuo doesn't need me. He has magnificent ears.

"Somebody's here," he says, panicking.

I feign alarm, stretch my neck. "Where? I can't see a bloody thing." He's right, of course. Councilman Yanaga has come to give his daily report. I smirk. Yanaga is a moron. I'm in love with his wife.

There's frenzy in his step. "Mitsuo," he says, "I cannot manage things. You must come to the office. Or we will have to move the registration here. No one will listen to me. It is impossible. Questionnaires have been stolen. We have used up our quota of pencils. Mr. Beardsly is adamant. He will not issue us new ones.

Mitsuo, we cannot register without pencils. Advise us."

Mitsuo assaults him.

"Fool, the Brothers have sentenced me to death, and you bother me with pencils. Did I leave a donkey in charge?" Instead of smarting or flinching, Yanaga comes to life. His face prickles with pleasure. "Mitsuo, I will get the pencils. I will make a bargain with Block 21."

He's about to go.

"Yanaga, how is Mimi?"

He would like to ignore my question.

"She has been transferred to a new department," he says, glum. "She is with Intake now."

"Intake? Is Swann planning to shuffle us around?"

He exchanges looks with Mitsuo. "I know nothing about it."

He leaves, and I return to my post at the window.

Took a break during Mitsuo's afternoon nap.

The canteen was overrun with babas. They occupied the dartboards, they lined up in front of the mirrors and plucked hair from their chins, they competed with their grandchildren for the attention of the countermen, demanding *aisukurimu* and *chokoleto*. I had nowhere to go.

Strolled behind the latrines.

Watched two old men fight over bathtub privileges.

Went for a nature hike.

Walked into the cactus in Block 32's rock garden.

Poked the ground for lizards.

The longer I walked the more depressed I grew. I'm too familiar with the terrain. I know where the snakes shed their skins. I keep maps of the ant trails in my head. I can tell how far the shadow from the nearest watchtower will creep on a sunny day. Not even the mountains amuse me. I know their contours by heart.

I went to Personnel. Told the Jap clerks I wanted a job. They laughed at me. "Anything," I said. "I'll blow up volleyballs. I'll knit sweaters. Swab the latrines." The head clerk advised me to go home. "We have nothing in your line, chief editor Tanaka."

"No titles, please. I'm serious. I'll take anything that's available."

"I'm sorry. We cannot issue you a work order. We do not have the authority."

"Dammit, can't you hear? I want to work. You issue work orders to everybody. Why am I a special case?"

The clerks scurried behind their gate. "I want to see the boss."

"Miss Wheat is not in today," the head clerk said. He didn't know what to do with me. He tried a threat. "You do not belong here. If you refuse to leave I will be forced to bring the policemen."

I kicked the gate and screamed. *"Eunice! Hey, Bunny!"*

The clerks were appalled at my behavior. A door

opened behind them. Bunny came out of her office. I made a horrible face at her. She wasn't put off by my evil looks. My anger only tickled her.

"Miss Wheat, I may be on Swann's shitlist, but I'm still entitled to a job. Why won't your clerks take my request?"

"Harold, what kind of job would you like?"

There was mockery in her voice, I'm sure. I decided to confound her, to make her stammer, to make her blush. I didn't take my eyes off her bosom.

"I want to work for Intake."

"You must be joking, Harold. Intake is practically defunct. They have a ghost corps. Two men. Are you expecting an exodus from another camp? We have no more room."

"Never mind. Just fill in the form. Intake."

"Come back at five, Harold. I'll see what I can do."

The clerks didn't leave until four forty-five.

Eunice didn't want to make love on her desk. She said it hurt her back. So we copulated standing up. We almost tripped. But my passion kept us anchored. We tore at each other, we kissed, we sucked, we chewed. After a while she grew alarmed.

Gallant, I said, "Should I stop?"

"Nooooo."

Ultimately her irony overcame her ardor, and she said, "Lover, are you trying to get a month's practice in one shot?"

I felt a chill on my backside, and I began to droop.

Eunice apologized. There was no need for it. Her reprimand was totally justified. The truth is, I hadn't given a thought to her in weeks. "Bunny, you've heard about my fall from grace. Swann has left me in the dumps. That's why I want a job."

Eunice was ready to re-establish good relations with me. She signed the work order and gave me my work button. "Intake?"

"Yes, Intake."

There was no one at Intake except two grumpy old men who squatted on the premises with brooms near their knees and seemed to be caretakers of some sort. They were mystified by my work order, and they stared shiftily at my button.

"Where's Mimi?"

"*Tabako ga aru?*" one of them said. He saw the cigarettes in my pocket. I gave him the whole pack. "Mimi. Miriam Yanaga."

They shrugged their shoulders and began fighting over the cigarettes.

"Intake," I said. "I'll kill Yanaga when I find him."

The Blood Brothers struck last night. Four of them, wearing cloaks, undressed Mitsuo while he was in the john, stepped on him, and told him it was only a warning. If the registration continued in his block, they would come back and take out his eyes. He grew dizzy after they left, fell, and bruised his head. Fumi took him to the hospital.

He scolded me in the morning.

"Harold, if you had accompanied me to the latrine they would not have dared to act. You had no right to abandon me." Sitting there in pajamas with wide sleeves, with a bandage on his head that had been wound in the shape of a turban, he looked like the Ottoman emperor in his royal bed. "Have you nothing to say to me?"

"Mitsuo, when are you coming home?"

"Are you a lunatic? I am staying at the hospital. My safety cannot be guaranteed anywhere else. Harold, you must speak to Mr. Haraguchi."

"What can old man Haraguchi do for you? Do you want him to organize a bachelors' brigade to fight the Brothers?"

"Don't be a fool, Harold. Haraguchi is the head of the Brothers. I'm sure of it. My councilmen have evidence. It could only be Haraguchi. Harold, he likes you. Go to him. Tell him I have no control over the registration."

"Mitsuo, I won't be your bagman. My days with the administration are over. There's an easier way out. Resign as block manager."

"Do you think that would stop them? Once your name is on the death list it can never be erased."

I'm a marked man.

Mitsuo's constituents consider me his surrogate, and

I can't play checkers or throw a dart without being sub-
jected to whole catalogues of petitions and woes. I don't
have Mitsuo's faculties. The complaints stick in my
head.

The bachelors' grievance committee cornered me at
home. They are fabulous breast-beaters, these old men.
They surrounded my bed and wept. Their lament lasted
a full hour. It gave me a headache, but it also wrenched
my heart. The young widows' club had appropriated a
tub from the men's washroom, and now the bachelors'
bath schedule has been thrown out of kilter. "Gentlemen," I said, "you must understand, I have no official
status. I'm only a private party. But I'll see what I can
do."

I argued the bachelors' case before the young widows.
They bristled at every mention of the tub, but Gordon
and I had always given them full coverage in the
Patriot, and the young widows were not ungrateful.
They had grievances of their own. The tub had orig-
inally belonged to them. They ordered it from Montgomery Ward and donated it to the women of our block.
But when the Blood Brothers demolished one of the
men's tubs during a raid on the washrooms, Maintenance
requisitioned the widows' tub and gave it to the bachelors, because they suffered the most. The young widows
sued for the tub's return, waited three weeks for Swann's
Justice Division to act, and then made their own justice.
They were furious. "Mesdames," I said, "right is clearly

on your side. Maintenance was rash. But the bachelors have an endless supply of stubbornness. They will plague the administration. They will hold a hunger strike. Swann will have to appease them. But perhaps there is another way."

Madam Hamada, president of the young widows, gave me a doubtful look. She wanted to know what my solution was.

"Half and half," I said.

"You speak in riddles, Harold. We cannot understand you."

"Half and half," I said. "The tub isn't stationary. It has already been transported once. Share it with the bachelors. We'll establish a shuttle system. You can have it back every second week."

The young widows took a vote. My proposal was carried by a very slim margin.

I sought Ruby's advice.

"Little sister, tell me where I can hide? I'm tired of playing King Solomon. The bachelors won't give me a moment's peace."

"Oniisan," she said, mimicking Fumi, "go to the gym."

"I've tried that. They follow me inside."

"Not today. The Jive Bombers are there. The old people hate the marathons. The stands will be deserted."

"Come with me, Ruby."

"No," she said. Her eyes flared. "It's boring. Wendell Haraguchi always wins. I hate the way he dances."

THE ONE AND ONLY JIVE BOMBERS, THE TRUE MIKADOS OF SWING FROM THE GILA RIVER RELOCATION CENTER, ARE WITH US UNDER THE AUSPICES OF THE US ARMY FOR THE SPECTACULAR ALL-DAY MANZANAR MARATHON DANCE IN HONOR OF THE FORMATION OF THE 442ND REGIMENTAL COMBAT TEAM.

The Jive Bombers, like all of us, have felt the pinch of war. They've been reduced to an ordinary eight-piece band. They did not create much of a stir with their makeshift music stands and borrowed trombones. There were only a dozen couples on the floor. The dancing was perfunctory. Each couple had its own trainer and an entourage of followers who were much more enthusiastic than the dancers themselves. Wendell and his partner, Miyo Harada, were escorted by twenty or so zootsuiters who made life miserable for everybody. They heckled the dancers, goosed the trainers, and intimidated the referee. Sergeant Sato sat in the judge's box guarding the winners' trophy. A few old women were scattered in the stands; most of them were asleep. Old man Haraguchi sat in the tier above me, munching peanuts, alone. It was obvious. He had come to clap for his nephew. I don't know how much truth there is in Mitsuo's accusations, and I don't care. Suppose the old man is the head of the Brothers. Even if he put me on his death list I would still have to be nice to him. He's the only link I have with my father. Dad won't speak to me. He claims I'm on Fumi's side. He doesn't believe that I'm impotent in all domestic matters. How could I upset the existing order at home? Fumi rules us all.

The old man bowed to me. I walked up to his tier.

Haraguchi Sensei is usually surrounded by his followers, but perhaps he didn't want to hurt Wendell's chances today and came to the marathon incognito. In any case, he offered me a peanut.

"Sensei, is my father well?"

"Indeed well, Harold. He is glowing. He cannot stop talking about you. I think you are in his favor again."

"Sensei, please, don't trifle with me."

"It is no joke, Harold. The reason is because of the tub. You are the new hero of the grievance committee. They say Unc' Haraguchi can do nothing for them, only you. They must take up all questions of a serious nature with Harold Sensei. Your father is very proud."

Haraguchi is a man of mystery. Nobody knows very much about his origins. His followers are tight-lipped about their master. But the bachelors love rumors, and they've spread an abundance of them. They say Unc' Haraguchi was the troublemaker of his village in Japan. He denounced the established religions and baited the local priests. He accused them of practicing mummery and milking the poor; one night, half drunk, he wrecked the village church. The priests demanded apologies and a new church. Haraguchi laughed at them, the story goes. He threatened to thrash them with a stick and appointed himself priest of his own church. The village chieftains could no longer tolerate him. He was beginning to threaten their authority. They imposed the dreaded *mura-hachibu*. Haraguchi was officially ostracized by the village. Anyone who spoke to him or helped him was to be beaten and fined. A few of the local farmers' sons who had come under Haraguchi's influence defied the decree of the chieftains and openly supported their master. Banished from the village, the farmers' sons emigrated to Hawaii, worked on the sugar plantations, saved their money religiously, came to the mainland, established themselves as truck farmers in the Salinas Valley, and sent for Haraguchi. Only one or two of them ever married. The rest have devoted themselves utterly to their Sensei. They live with him in the dorm. They are all old men, some with crooked backs, arthritic elbows, or weak hearts, but I'm sure that if Swann tampered with their Sensei, all the military policemen in the world wouldn't be able to save him.

We sat, cracking peanut shells, and watched the marathon progress. Five couples had already been eliminated. Wendell danced without bothering to shuffle his feet. Miyo slept on his shoulder. He didn't want to disturb her. He ordered the zootsuiters to make a little less noise.

"Sensei, Mitsuo sends his greetings from the hospital. You must have heard about his accident. He got in the way of some gnomes who haunt the men's latrine. He says the gnomes have persuaded him to give up politics."

Sensei laughed. "Harold, tell Mitsuo he will soon be safe. Swann-san is getting rid of the gnomes."

"Eh Sensei?"

"The No-Noes will be removed from camp. Swann-san intends to force us out."

"Sensei, Swann wouldn't dare. That's crazy. It's probably a rumor. Swann has learned from the bachelors. He's trying to work up some enthusiasm for his resettlement program. The camps are becoming too costly for the government."

"No, no. It is a certainty. We will be removed."

Wendell overcame his torpor for a moment and waved to his uncle. The zootsuiters seized the opportunity. They implored the other dancers to show more respect to Unc' Haraguchi. One couple collapsed while trying to wave and was immediately disqualified from the competition. Haraguchi stood up and bowed. The zootsuiters whistled and stamped their feet. Shells spilled from the old man's pockets during the din and floated down to the tier below.

Sensei's prophecy came true.
Danny Hayashi brought out a special edition of the

Patriot two days later. I shivered when I saw the words "loyal" and "disloyal." The purge was on.

Swann was magnanimous. He was willing to give the recalcitrants one more chance. Each of them had an additional ninety-six hours in which to change from a No-No to a Yes-Yes. Otherwise they would be declared "disloyal" and put on "segregation lists," together with those evacuees who had requested repatriation to Japan or who had failed to cooperate with WRA and the Army by not filling out the registration forms. "All disloyal evacuees are potential threats to the security of the United States," and would have to be "segregated from the loyal evacuees who are contributing to the war effort." Disloyals from each of the camps would be shipped to Tule Lake, which was being converted into a special WRA "segregation center." On the other hand, all loyal Tuleans would be redistributed to the remaining nine loyal camps.

I have to admit that I panicked. Gordon wasn't around to advise me, to pommel me, to pull my hair. I shot across the firebreak, alarming the old women in my wake. There was a crowd outside Mitsuo's office. I ran to the head of the line. The door was closed. I banged. "Open. I want to register. Right now. You hear?" Councilman Yanaga peeked out the window. "Harold," he said, "you will have to wait. There will be a delay. We did not expect such a rush. We are short of registration forms."

He must have seen the demons in my face. He opened up without another word of protest. Fumiko was inside. She was amazed by my newfound zeal.

Next I made a beeline for Intake. My intuition didn't fail me. The place was crawling with Jap porters, secretaries, and petty officers. I had no trouble finding out who was in charge. Beardsly pushed and poked people with his truncheon and shouted absurd, contradictory orders, which helped him keep calm and were meant for no one but himself. His Jap force acted on each of his orders and began dropping file cabinets and banging into one another. Still, Beardsly's truncheon kept things under control. He growled when he saw me. "Harold, what do you want?"

I showed him my work button. At first he thought it was a fake. He threatened me with the truncheon. "If you're here for trouble, you monkey, you've come to the right place." He searched me and found my work order. It enraged him. He knew it was bona fide. "Personnel must be ready for suicide," he said. He made me sit in the corner. Then, suddenly, unpredictably, his attitude changed. He picked me up by the lapels. "Did you come here to sit on your ass? Work, man, work. The colony will be flooded with new evacuees in a couple of weeks. Each one of them will come through Intake. We have to be prepared."

I swept a little, I unloaded file cabinets, I cut out name tags, I made a sign or two, I looked for Mimi.

Between the cabinets and the swishing brooms I caught a glimpse of her delicate shoulders and her plump derriere. To be truthful, I froze. The absolute beauty of her ass overwhelmed me. I shook, I began to sweat. It's love, nothing less. It's made a monster of me. I can't remember the exact number of times I've wished for Yanaga's death. I swear I'd murder him myself if it would bring me closer to Mimi. Nothing would help. Mimi won't have anything to do with me. She was my assistant once. She wrote articles for me. She corrected copy. I gave her orders, I charmed her, I made her cry, I wooed her in subtle, roundabout ways, without a kiss or a delicate touch; she would have been my mistress by and by, but I couldn't control my lusts. I planned my villainy a week in advance. On target day I dismissed my two secretaries and sent Gordon to the other end of camp; certain that Yanaga was at a council meeting, I summoned Mimi, feigned excitement over a new idea she had for an article, plied her with marshmallow bars, beer, and saké, ignored her, complimented her, yawned in her face, told her jokes and made her giddy, and finally seduced her, raped her, whatever you will. She's avoided me ever since.

I felt a sharp pain in my kidneys. Beardsly was being free with his truncheon. "Are we paying you to dream?" he said. I ducked behind a cabinet and ran over to Mimi. She turned her head away.

"Mimi, Miriam, please. I don't ask for much. Just smile, say hello, and I'll leave you alone forever."

She gave me a broom. "Sweep and shut up."

Overjoyed, I said, "Mimi, say something else."

"If you come near me, Harold Tanaka, you'll have the stockade to think about."

"More," I said. "More." The angry lines around her chin, her fierceness, her chilliness aroused me. "Mimi." Mimi walked away.

It was useless trying to work. I snuck out of Intake and made my way to Personnel. The Jap clerks weren't very friendly. I walked through their gate without bowing or asking permission.

Eunice was eating a sandwich in her office. She didn't smile. "Have you come for another work order? Sorry, Swann is cracking down. No more jobs for retired editors. Unless you want to deliver newspapers for Danny Hayashi."

"Bunny," I said, "get undressed."

"Don't be funny, Hal." I didn't have to preen for her. She put away the sandwich. "Harold, for God's sake, you avoid me for weeks at a time, and then, when you get the urge, I'm supposed to drop everything and fuck for you with my clerks outside the door."

"Right," I said. "Get undressed."

In the middle of all the furor, with Mitsuo in the hospital and Fumiko spending her days supervising the registration in our block, Ruby gave birth to a boy. As the oldest son in the family, I put myself in charge. I named the baby Benjamin Lazarus Tanaka. Madam Arakaki, Block 18's *uranaishi*, made an unfortunate prediction while she was drunk: any bastard boy child born in the Year of the Monkey would damn us all. The bachelors howled. They were the ones who kept Madam Arakaki in business. They believed that all fortune-tellers were infallible. The bachelors crouched outside my window and wouldn't go away until I confronted Madam Arakaki. I threatened her, I did. "You windbag, you got your calendar mixed up. This is the Year of the Sheep. I'll choke you to death if you don't change your mind about the baby." Madam Arakaki apologized. I greased her palm with a two-dollar bill. She reversed her prediction and assured the bachelors that baby-san was a blessing rather than a curse. The bachelors rejoiced.

The secret societies have countered Swann's segregation proclamation with measures of their own. At least ten death lists have been circulating around camp; the lists are composed primarily of block managers and council members. Councilman Yanaga is on eight of them; Mitsuo's on all ten.

The day after Swann's proclamation Mitsuo's office was packed with late registrants and recanting No-Noes. Evacuees began to shun the office during the following afternoon; and by the end of the second day the registration came to a halt. It's true the Blood Brothers had declared all managers' offices *inu* territory, but it wasn't only threats that kept the evacuees away. Neither was it Haraguchi Sensei's presence, nor Professor Ifukube's rantings. It was Toshio.

Before the segregation proclamation Toshio was simply an agitator, a cook, and the leader of the Kibei; now he's a prophet. Professor Ifukube invades our block with his two sumo champions and his gang of fanatics; he shouts, he threatens, he damns WRA, and the people flee from him. Toshio comes alone, without aides, without an army of bodyguards; he doesn't exhort, he doesn't advise; he listens, he soothes. An old man tells him: "Toshio, I have a son in the Japanese Army. *Shikata na gai.* It can't be helped. If I say Yes-Yes, what will happen to my son? I must go to Tule, *ne? Shikata na gai.*" Toshio will touch the old man's shoulder and repeat: "*Shikata na gai.*" Perhaps he'll also say: "Father, go to Tule."

A few weeks ago a group of Nisei raided the headquarters of Seinen-Kai, the Kibei young men's association at camp, and denounced Toshio and all the Kibei. Today the same group of Nisei flock to Toshio. "My old man says there's no future for him in America. He wants to take the family to Tule. But I can't go with him, Toshio. Can you imagine me in Tokyo after the war? I'm staying here." Toshio will nod. "Do honor to your father. Even if you cannot obey him. Tell him the way you feel. Do not allow him to leave in anger."

The bachelors haven't been idle; they've been composing stories about Toshio's past and recounting them throughout camp. Ten years ago Toshio was a zootsuiter in Fresno, the bachelors say. To cure him of his dissolute habits, his uncle removed him from school and sent him to study in Japan. When he returned three years later he gave up his pegged pants, his T-shirts, his long coat, and his widebrimmed hat. He worked in a Jap noodle shop, delivered lectures in the service of Lord Buddha, and organized the Kibei of Fresno.

After the evacuation Toshio and the other Kibei had a hard time. Nobody at Manzanar trusted them. They were too American for the Issei, and for the Nisei they were too Japanese; so they kept to themselves. They had their own organizations, their own occupations. A Kibei was invariably a cook or a construction worker. The isolation from the rest of the camp hurt and angered the Kibei, made them sullen and suspicious, but it paid an unexpected dividend. The Kibei soon controlled the kitchen and construction crews, and they became the one effective political force at camp. While the Issei moaned over Swann's successive proclamations and the Nisei floundered, the Kibei met, held protests, and threatened to strike or sabotage their own work. The Kibei have few seats on the block councils; the block managers call them troublemakers; the children avoid them; the old women spit at them; yet whatever concessions Swann has made, he's made because of the Kibei.

Swann's latest proclamation has altered the state of camp affairs. The popularity of the Kibei has risen overnight. The young Nisei men who have considered themselves American in spite of their present home, who have held War Bond rallies, denounced the Kibei, volunteered for Prudhomme's combat unit, see their fathers preparing to pack for Tule and wonder about their identity for the first time. Old Issei men who have requested repatriation, who say they have no ties with America, who dream of the *takura-bune,* the great treasure ship from Japan that will bring them home, are stunned when they realize that their youngest sons and daughters may not accompany them to Tule. The Kibei no longer seem strange or out of place. Issei and Nisei have been made aware that the peculiar restlessness of the Kibei, the agony of being able to feel neither American nor Japanese, is now their own.

Fumiko's frustrations over Chuichi have turned her into a fury. Chuichi drinks saké with the Kibei cooks, he holds constant dialogues with Toshio, he disappears for days at a time and comes back with bruises and a bloody shirt, but Fumi says nothing to him. I'm the one who has to pay.

If I fall asleep, she wakes me. If I stay up, she scolds

me, she pinches me in bed, she reminds me of her prowess with a broom. I long for the olden times, when I spent my days and nights in my office, arguing with Gordon or charting the seduction of one councilman's wife or another.

"Oniisan," she says in the middle of my dream, "you must find Chuichi. Mr. Swann is taking his curfew seriously again. Chuichi will be in trouble."

Drowsy, I grope for my slippers and bathrobe.

I yawn. "Nesan, where is he?"

She pokes me in the ribs. "He's with the cooks. Find him and bring him home. Talk to him, Harold. You are his older brother. Tell him he must not go to Tule. He will break up the family. We must stay together for Mother's sake. Tell him."

I'm about to scratch, but I know my impertinence will cost me plenty, so I wait until I'm outside. I'm naked under my robe, and I have to hug myself to keep warm. Chuichi.

I'm three years older, but Chuichi was my classmate all through grammar school. We went to a two-room schoolhouse outside Watsonville. There were fifteen-year-old Italians, hotheaded Filipinos with battle scars and fancy knives, and six-year-old Japanese girls in the same class. Chuichi was our savior. He was scrawny and his nose always ran, but I've seen him destroy three Guineas at a time by battering them with his elbows and his head. The Fils had great fun carving each other up, but they kept their knives in their pockets when Chuichi was around. Fifteen boochies, we marched to school with Chuichi at the head of the line. Half of us were older than he was, and when we were alone with him we made fun of the way he sniffled and couldn't blow his nose, we bullied him, we heckled him, but as soon as a Guinea or a Fil appeared, Chuichi took charge, and his grimaces kept up our courage and prevented us from whining and shaking and peeing in our pants.

I track toward the latrine, still hugging myself.

Whoever's afoot, I want to give them warning of my whereabouts, so I whistle. My song is misinterpreted. An iron hand shoots out of the latrine, grips my robe, and whisks me inside. I trip, and two, three men kick me and pull the robe over my head. They hiss and call me spy. My bare ass touches the slimy floor. I shudder, but I don't move. "Chuichi," I cry. "Came for Chuichi. Hope to die."

Can't see any faces, but I take a chance. "Chuichi, it's only me. Sis wants you to go to bed."

Somebody picks me up and helps me put on my robe.

Beardsly's become a tyrant.

He makes us report at six a.m. and we rehearse all day for the arrival of refugees from Tule. Beardsly divides us into companies and teams. Some of us play refugee, others remain Intake officers, and the rest sit on the sidelines and watch. Beardsly's our impresario. He's the master of the show. Today I'm a loyal Tulean. I hunch my back, I whine, I squint, I snatch Beardsly's briefcase, handle it roughly, and carry it around like a bindle. Beardsly throws scowls at me, but he doesn't want to stop the games. The Intake officers push us and make us form an orderly line. I resist. I hop in front of the officers. "Yaaaaah." I address my compatriots. "Brothers, they say there are snakes and pickpockets at Manzanar. Watch where you step. We're in an evil place." Mimi's on the sidelines. She ignores my performance. Beardsly accuses me of overacting. I bow. "Sorry, Monroe-san." But I keep it up. "Yaaah, yaaah." I tease the officers. I toss my bindle in the air. The clasps open, and Beardsly's papers begin to scatter. I rush to retrieve them, but it's too late. The truncheon falls. I protect my head. "Play with me," Beardsly says. "Teach you." He drubs my lower back. "Next time you'll learn not to interfere." I crawl over to the sidelines. My eyeglasses come off. Squinting, I make out the color of Mimi's dress. Are there tears in her eyes? Can't tell. "Fool," she says. "Have you lost your dignity, Harold?"

"Never had any."

"He'll make you pay a heavy price for your buffoonery."

"It's worth it." The hell with love. I vow to bang her again no matter what.

"Perhaps," she says, "you were always meant to crawl about on your knees." Beardsly pages her. He doesn't want Mimi to be contaminated by me. He puts her in charge of the games. Without me, my team is on its best behavior. The officers distribute fake name tags. Intake proceeds without a hitch.

I crawl outside. No one offers to help. Too absorbed in the games. Feel the welts on my back. I can't stand up. I leave my eyeglasses off. I'll be a blind man for a while. Why bother to see? My visions startle the void. Trees uproot themselves for me. Barracks shimmy. Cactus spines catch fire. But there's little I can do about the cinders on the ground. They bite into elbow, palm, and knee. I crawl sideways. The traffic must be heavy. I bump into somebody. He refuses to budge. "Do you have to confuse a blind man? Get out of the way." I wax arrogant, with my knees on the ground and my ass in the air. I sniff at him with great scorn. His odor wreaks vengeance on my bones. I shake from tip to toe. I fumble for my glasses. He slaps them away.

"Gordon, what are you doing here?"

"Meditating."

"In the middle of the road? I've been looking for you for weeks. You crazy, I saw your name on the segregation lists. Are you trying to pull a joke on Swann? His head has no room for humor. He'll think you're serious."

"I am. I'm going to Tule."

"Gordon, find my specs, quick. How can I throttle you if I can't see?"

He fits the glasses abruptly on my face. His fingers press against my forehead. There's no compassion in his touch. He's wearing soiled pajamas. The sleeves are torn. Scratches on his arm. Dark ridges near his cheeks. His eyes are dull. His motions are clumsy. He moves without energy or grace.

"I've changed my mind. I won't throttle you. I'm going to cart you off to Swann's psycho ward for observation. *Tule*. What will you do there? Be Professor Ifukube's aide? Gordon, I thought our separation hurt me the most. I was wrong. You're lost without me. Lost. You hear? I won't let you go to Tule. Never."

He jumps up and down and makes a fist. "Ninny," he says. "Worthless ninny. Stay, Harold. You belong here. Beardsly needs someone to pick up his droppings. You will make a perfect dung collector."

"Don't go too far with me, Gordon. Better give me some advice. Should I go to Tule with you and wait for the treasure ship to come? We would make a good pair in Tokyo, you and I. We'll sell fish along the Ginza and do a comedy act. We'll be loved by one and all. Yes, I will stay here. I'd rather eat Beardsly's dung than listen to the professor."

"I have nothing to do with Ifukube. I am going with the Kibei."

"I see." I crawl around him, declaring my petulance. "I see. The Kibei have converted you. You've joined

Toshio's flock. Soon you'll be saying prayers to the Emperor and waving a Nihonjin flag. Gordon, I don't care what ceremonies they've put you through. Even if they've made you a Blood Brother, you're not a yabo, and you never will be. Don't pretend, Gordon. We're no different. Swann can lock me in a cage for all I care. Rights? Privileges? Let him keep them. Manzanar means nothing to me. I've become a zombie since I'm at camp. I have no heart, no blood. Pinch me, nothing happens. I'm stiff as a board. That's the only way."

"Harold, you've made a mistake. Your suspended animation isn't voluntary. It's Swann who has put you on ice. Be careful. You may wake up one day to discover that being a zombie is a permanent affair."

Gordon's bitterness has enacted a miraculous cure. My back no longer pains me. I get up. Gordon is ready to leave. Desperate, afraid, I demand some attention and step on his foot. "Should I show you what a zombie can do?" With his head half turned, he pushes me in the face. He has no hate, no love, no anger left for me. Only disgust. Only disgust.

The bachelors have a new complaint.

Wendell has left them in the lurch. He refuses to supply them with French decks. I'm not surprised. Wendell has become a militant. He's given up his zoot suit. He wears a student's cap and a work shirt, and he's cut off most of his hair. He distributes his uncle's pamphlets and lectures us on Japan's crusade to free the colored people of the world. Expecting rewards, the bachelors have become Wendell's claque. They badger grandmothers and little boys into attending the lectures, they sing Wendell's praises, they clap for him, they publicize his lecture routes, but Wendell gives them nothing.

I can commiserate with the old men. I understand their loss. Wendell's decks are extraordinary. I have one. You wouldn't believe the number of sexual acts that two people might perform until you have seen my cards. The same couple, a short man with a mustache and hairy legs and a woman with imperfect skin, labor in all fifty-two cards plus the two jokers. Don't think their performance is haphazard or shoddy. If you arrange the cards according to suits, you will find that fellatio is hearts' theme; diamonds is devoted to cunnilingus; anal intercourse is practiced exclusively in clubs; and spades is a mixed bag of tricks. I have great sympathy for the performers. The man carries a bored expression throughout the deck, even in the most intimate of poses; and his perpetual erection is more of a curse than a blessing for his partner; her waxen features and astonished eyes belie her agility and her prowess; in several of the poses she seems quite close to hysteria. Of course I may be wrong. A marvelous effect can be introduced by flipping the deck. The frozen quality of the individual poses is obscured; and the performers, now animated, seem much more eager to perform.

Visited Mitsuo in the hospital again. He was in a terrible state. The Blood Brothers had broken in the night before and had rampaged through the hospital, haranguing patients, threatening evacuee doctors and nurses, stealing urine specimens, denouncing the block councils, and forecasting the death of every block manager and council member at camp. Mitsuo ran next door to the TB ward and hid there.

"Harold, it was a plot to murder me. I was lucky. I know how superstitious the Japanese are about tuberculosis. They would not dare enter the TB ward. I watched them through the glass door. Some of them wore pillowcases over their heads. I recognized the two who ransacked my bed. One was Wendell. The other was Hiroshi. Haraguchi has poisoned them all." He clutched my sleeve. "Harold, do you understand? My own assistant was prepared to murder me. I can trust no one. No one."

The managers and councilmen besieged Swann with petitions, declarations, and affidavits: the incident at the hospital, they declared, was conclusive evidence that the administration could no longer protect them from hoodlums, agitators, and spies. Swann offered to remove them to an abandoned prison farm near Death Valley until he conducted a more thorough investigation. Their children and wives would not be allowed to accompany them. Councilman Yanaga was one of the first to leave. Mitsuo elected to remain at camp. He had no confidence in Swann's proposal. "Death Valley? There are poisonous spiders in Death Valley. I will take my chances here."

The Army engineers are building a fence around the Caucasian living quarters. Swann was opposed to it, but his own men threatened to strike unless he gave them their fence. They are afraid the No-Noes will commit some sabotage before they are sent to Tule. They've grown suspicious of all evacuees. Bunny says she's about to resign. She has daily fantasies of being raped by her own clerks. I tell her not to worry. "Swann's been putting saltpeter in the soup." Funny thing, my news doesn't seem to console her. She pulls a long face and tells me she has work to do.

Trouble at home. Fumiko's resigned herself to losing Chuichi, but she has no intention of giving Napoleon to Tule. Napoleon has rolled his Sea Scout middy into a bindle and is waiting for Swann's bus to take him away. "Chuichi," he says. "I'm going with Chuichi." Fumi snatches at his hair in desperation. "Little fool, Tule Lake is the land of the dead. No one will survive it." Should I contradict her? Nesan, you give Swann-san too much credit. His relocation program does not deserve to be mythologized. Tule is Tule. I would provide Napoleon with much more practical reasons for remaining here, but his bindle and his anxious looks disband my arguments and drive me from home.

Swann has made a concession to his white personnel. He's rounded up Professor Ifukube and five token Kibei and dispatched them to Tule in a station wagon a few days before the official departure day. Haraguchi Sensei wasn't touched. Swann must have understood that if his men dragged Sensei away from his dorm, they would have had to fight a war with the bachelors. The roundup was a failure nonetheless. The Caucasians still want their fence. And the rest of the camp is in an ugly mood.

Intake is preparing for all contingencies. Beardsly has appointed a squad of white policemen to be our supervisors. The policemen are as bored as we are. They fall asleep when Beardsly isn't around. Or else they take turns trying to proposition Mimi. The Jap clerks and petty officers despise councilman Yanaga and don't give a damn about his wife, so it's up to me, Mimi's ex-ravisher, to preserve her virtue. The policemen have their clubs and their evil tempers, but what do I care? I take action against them all as soon as one of them goes near Mimi. I stick out my tongue, I wag my behind, I bray at them. "Baaaa, brothers. Find another bone to play with. Baaaaa." My braying has an effect. It rattles them, and they forget Mimi for a while. They trip me, they pull my ears, they jab me with their sticks, but not too hard. You see, I have a protector now. Beardsly's been good to me of late. He's relying on me to save his show. He's made me a petty officer. I'm supposed to greet the loyal Tuleans when the big day comes and take them through Intake. And the policemen are aware of what Beardsly will do to them if I'm maimed or disfigured, so they go easy on me.

Mimi is the one who is most disturbed by my behavior. She knows my jousts with the policemen are in her behalf, and though she has some contempt for me she doesn't have the heart to ignore my chivalry. There are signals of confusion in her face. She has anger on her brow, alarm under her eyes, and pity near her mouth. And love is somewhere too. Or is it simply loneliness? No matter. If I followed her home I'm sure I could find a way to tickle her quim. Something's wrong with me. I have no desire to rape Mimi, seduce her even. Perhaps my saltpeter story is true. Swann's unmanned us all.

His moans sent shivers through me, and we cried together while I struggled with him, but I couldn't let Napoleon go. "Chuichi . . ." Ruby sat on his legs, Fumi bit her nails, and little Benjamin Lazarus wailed in his crib. "Poleon, they won't let you wear your uniform at Tule Lake. No more Sea Scouts. Good-by. You'll have to join the Japanese Navy. Is that what you want? They'll cut your hair. Make you salute the Emperor. Stay here.

With us, Poleon." Looked out the window. Swann's pickup truck was in front of the barracks. Sensei and his devotees, eight old men in pajamas and pea coats who huddled around their master to keep him warm, Toshio and his cooks, Chuichi, Wendell, Gordon, Hiroshi, two young men, an old couple from our block who had elected to return to Japan, and their eldest daughter, an ugly girl who liked to sneer, were all on board. I saw another face. Standing among the cooks, with his head partly obscured by Wendell's bobbing cap, was Spider Sam. I yelped. Napoleon began to bite, scratch, and kick, and I had to pinion him and avoid his snapping jaws. "Fumi, I can't hold him. I have to save Sam." Fumi gathered rags, shoelaces, and Mitsuo's old shirts, and we tied Napoleon to the bed.

Quarreled with the driver. "Sam Yoshima. He doesn't belong up there." The two MPs who were guarding the truck told the driver to move on. I tried to climb aboard. The MPs clubbed me to the ground. Ugly daughter laughed. Gordon looked me in the eye. The truck drove off.

Cornered Beardsly at Intake. I was out of breath. Dug my fingers inside his shirt cuffs and tugged his sleeves. He was about to call the police. "Monroe, Sam Yoshima was picked up. His name isn't on the segregation lists. You can't take him to Tule."

He had nothing to say about Sam. Told me to get my fucking claws out of his sleeves.

"If you don't get Spider released, I swear, Monroe, I'll demolish Intake. I'll break your fixtures. I'll foul your window sills. I'll chew your walls. I'll pee, I'll shit, I'll devour."

Beardsly signed an order forbidding Spider to leave camp, gave it to me, and kicked me out of his office. "You come back here again, you lunatic, I'll lock you up. Keep away."

The bastards made me run. Every time I came near, the truck pulled away. I waved Beardsly's order, I shouted obscenities about the driver's mother, I challenged the MPs to a fight, I couldn't catch the truck. The driver took delight in torturing me. He drove in circles. I was dizzy, I was nauseous, I had stomach cramps and Charley horses, and on my fourth trip around the firebreak the eaves of the barracks seemed terribly sharp and pinched the nerves in my head, windows gleamed and turned black, chimney smoke crossed the horizon in a curlicue, I fell down. MPs helped me up. Driver offered me a seat in his cab. I read Beardsly's order to him. MPs lowered the tailboard for me. Climbed up, up. I was jostled and shoved by Sensei's men. Bristling with hostility, ugly daughter unbuttoned my fly. I shoved her against the cooks and dragged Sam out from under Sensei's pea coat. I knew I would have to be firm with him. "Sam, Sam, what will you do in Tule? You never liked the Kibei. Who will you have? Napoleon isn't going." Sam picked me up. He carried me away from the tailboard and into the heart of the truck. I never realized how deep a truck could be. It was windy in there. Dust blew in my eyes, and I got a chill. The cooks had their hands under ugly daughter's skirt. Sensei's tongue was in her mouth. Daughter moved her torso in rhythm with the cooks' probing hands, she even sighed, but she kept her sneer. Gordon, Hiroshi, and Wendell crowded around us. Their intentions were most ambiguous. They smiled, they stroked my hair, they grabbed me, they pushed Sam out of the way. They socked me, they abused me, they tore my shirt, they tossed me overboard.

Oh, I went through all the motions. On Monday 127 souls passed through my station. We examined their scalps and armpits for lice, we gave them name tags, barracks numbers, and toothbrushes. The men were suspicious, the women and children were frightened. They carried suitcases, bundles, and sticks of furniture. We reassured those who were gloomy, we dispelled rumors about the prevalence of the Black Dragon Society at Manzanar, we told the loyal Tuleans not to worry: every No-No had been weeded out. I was hearty, I was gracious, I didn't covet any housewives or their daughters, I patted shoulders, I kissed babies, I gave out cupcakes, I repacked suitcases, I repaired broken chairs, I offered my services for free. Beardsly was testy in the morning, but he was buoyant by the middle of the day. He shook my hand, he called me Hal, he told me the whole administration was talking about my rehabilitation. He winked, he nudged me in private, he said the word was that Danny Hayashi might step down from the *Patriot*. I was harsh with him. "Monroe, I have no time for small talk. Can't you see I'm busy?" He apologized and winked again. Mimi wanted to have lunch with me. I said no. Yanaga and the other councilmen were back from Death Valley, but it didn't matter. My good works made her bosom swell. I ignored her all day.

On Tuesday we processed an additional 97 souls. I asked one soul who smelled of politics and had indeed been a block manager at Tule if he knew anything about the condition of the Manzanar No-Noes. "Those dogs," he said. "They belong in that hell-hole." He saw the face I made, and without any further speculation he shifted his point of view. "The Manzanar brothers are doing well, captain. Very, very well." I would have kicked him, but I was afraid the other Tuleans on line might panic, and Beardsly's spotless Intake record would be ruined. So I gave him his toothbrush and let him go.

I lost my appetite for checking lice. I questioned everybody. "Gordon Nishitsujii. He's short and ferocious and he never smiles. And my brother Chuichi, Chuichi Tanaka, formerly of the US Infantry. It shows in the way he dresses. He has a field jacket and combat boots. Have you seen them?" The Tuleans thought I was mad. They were reluctant to submit to my scalp inspections. Beardsly wanted to take me away from my

station. "Hal, you need a rest." I told him I was fine.
An old man with a dirty scalp was eager to answer my
questions. "They're dead. Don't you know? The Army's
making Tule into an extermination camp. We were the
last ones to get out. Believe me, your brother's dead."
Did I choke him? I don't remember. I did scream though.
"Murderers, murderers." Policemen held my arms. Mimi
washed my face. Beardsly soothed the Tuleans. "It's
nothing. Back on line, please. My assistant has been
working too hard." He sent me home.

Or ?world the Destroy ?life in aim Devil's the What's
-be true only the Devil's the Nowadays ?Name His sanctify
.beast or man for place no Manzanar's .him Trust .liever
-Be .cocoon a in nights and days our spend to ought We
is fart a says Gordon .cacodaemon a and coconut a tween
the or best the Does .character man's a to key the
.know don't I ?underwear his foul worst

Mitsuo's out of the hospital. Thinks it's safe. He ought
to sniff the wind. There's malice in the air. He won't
find any peace. Block managers are no longer valuable.
He'll have to leave or pick rags like the rest of us.

Manzanar 1943

AP, IP, & UP

Cocksure and cuntshy Harold Tanaka, former Nisei
Man of the Hour, was caught *flagrante delicto* last
Thursday performing an unnatural caress on the person

of an undisclosed female WRA official and is now being held in seclusion at the county courthouse in Independence. The reaction of the entire colony is one of horror and shame. Tanaka has been charged with conduct unbecoming a colonist of Manzanar, with gross violation of American womanhood, with sedition and sexual dereliction. In an exclusive interview before his arraignment, Tanaka said: "Cuntwise, we are what we eat." He later retracted this statement. Judge J. Arch Volpo of the municipal court called Tanaka a liar, a fiend, a vile bugbear, a depraved brute, a Jap rat, and a discredit to his race, and refuses to release him on his own recognizance, though Tanaka has sworn to curb his tongue.

My socks have lost elasticity. Fumi's washings are to blame: is it the hard water here or the hot weather? They droop around my ankles, and I trip because of them, but they give me the look of a clown and help me entertain Napoleon, who hasn't smiled since we held him down and let the bus to Tule escape without him. Can a body be in one place and its spirit in another? Little brother's made of wood. I poke him on the head. "Poleon, Poleon, come play with me." No response. I shake him good and hard, put an ear over his heart, and listen for some music. Nothing. His spirit's fled. Did you know Poleon's a true son of Nihon? Mom crossed the Great Ocean in 1927 to visit her sick father while she was carrying Poleon, and he was born in Tokyo, under the watchful eye of Mount Fuji. When the Spanish consul, Count Alfonso Rojas de Amado, comes to Manzanar to look after the rights of all Japanese nationals, he snubs Fumi and me, but he has booklets for Napoleon embossed with the Emperor's seal. Napoleon hides under his bed during Count Alfonso's semiannual visit to the barracks. He doesn't want to be reminded of the circumstances of his birth. After all, he only spent his first three weeks out of the womb in Japan, no more. And what would the Emperor do if he heard about Poleon's Sea Scout middy? So I poke him again. "Poleon, Count Alfonso's here." It's a lie, but I have to find a way to animate him. Nothing doing. Only Chuichi, I'm afraid, could recall him to life.

I've been indicted again. Dammit, Bunny's turned state's witness. It isn't exactly rape. It's a pale dot on a thin line. Good Nisei girls, I'm told, are afraid to take walks after dark because of me. Your cock will be your downfall, that's what Bunny said. Obviously it isn't true. Am I the loco cunnilinguist who traveled through the orphans' dormitory at midnight and licked the vital zones of a dozen pubescent girls in one great swoop? I can't deny it, my sexual habits aren't pure. Does Swann have conclusive evidence, or is it a trumped-up charge, meant to humiliate me, to put me out of business for a while? Blackstone isn't around to interrogate me, why? The War Department has whisked him away. He's the new master of Tule. They need him. Tule's been turned into an experimental station to prepare for the occupation of Japan. The former Tuleans who have settled comfortably here sit on freshly painted porches and talk of the curious building program that began a week before they left. "The Army engineers shut the factories and fixed them up with brand-new smokestacks." Smokestacks? Are you sure? Anybody notice the color of the soot? Did it have a greenish-blue iridescence, the telltale glow of charred human flesh? "Troublemaker," they said. "Fascist stooge, red dog, go on, scram." You see, I know too much. Swann had to put me away.

Been working on a comedy. An operetta to be exact. Something light, something gay, with costumes, scenery, and lace, to celebrate our life at Manzanar, to prove once and for all that Japanese Americans aren't fraught with hysteria and prone to morbidity. We intend to scrub our faces before we go on stage, wash our armpits, rinse our private parts. We'll be so clean, the administration will love us. I'm hoping Swann will let us go on tour. The Merry Maid of Manzanar, or Dry Atlantis, a comic extravaganza in three parts, about a new utopia in the desert, circa 1942, by Harold Togo Tanaka, with a little help from Aristophanes, Plato, Sir Thomas More, and Benjamin of Gonzaga. Won't be any problems with casting. Everybody plays himself in my comedy. Why shouldn't Swann play Swann? He has fiery speeches and free sway. Am I to blame if the Merry Maid, whom Swann has been lusting after for two and three-quarters acts, turns out to be a man? The plot's banal, I admit. The new utopia, under Swann, has very strict rules; it's only for the straight and the good. The world outside is racked with war and pestilence and riotous sex; girls are attacked by their own fathers; brother fights brother; cannibalism is the order of the day. People clamor to get into Manzanar; applications have passed the one-million mark. A delegation has come to petition Swann. Swann appears at the main gate. He's wearing a kerchief over his nose; he wants no contact with the outsiders. "We don't accept the dissolute, we have no room for the depraved." While Swann issues his rebuke we have a pastoral scene within the gate. Five lovely Nisei girls harnessed together with garlands of flowers and leaves, wearing diaphanous silk gowns with nothing underneath, sing our anthem, "Sweet, Sweet Manzanar," swing their hips with great discretion, and toss nosegays over the gate. The delegation goes wild; the men froth, play with themselves, play with one another, and beg Swann to let them in. "Nothing doing," says Swann. He has his tower guards pepper the ground around the delegation with machine-gun fire. Meanwhile, unbeknownst to Swann, a member of the delegation slips through the rear gate, left unguarded because of the commotion. Aware that he will be butchered on sight if discovered, he assumes the disguise that he has brought with him: wig, false breasts, buttock plates, clip-on female genitals, thigh putty, and peekaboo sheath. Bold, unbelievably daring, he sprints across the length and breadth of the camp and joins the flower chain of girls still dancing for Swann's amusement near the main gate. Does Swann notice the new arrival? You bet! The Merry Maid jogs one of his false breasts, causes his buttock plates to ripple, and does such delightful things with his put-on genitals, Swann moans aloud. He knows he will have the Merry Maid to himself. You see, all the men at Manzanar, save Swann, are eunuchs. Swann's had their organs anesthetized. That's the price they've had to pay to enter. Swann wasn't counting on a female impersonator to destroy his idyll. And while he pursues the Merry Maid in Acts One and Two, the Maid himself, feigning simple curiosity, inspects, fondles, and kisses the labia majora and minora of every girl at camp in the community tub. I don't intend to disclose the grand finale. All I can say is that Swann is ousted in a bloodless coup, and the Merry Maid gets to be the king-queen of Manzanar. Simple, perfect, but something's wrong. Only one man alive can play the Merry Maid: Gordon. And he's so damn far away.

Had a visitor. Mimi. Whole camp was at the magic show. Lord Mertan of Hollywood was performing in the amphitheatre. In spite of the ordinary fare—rabbits launched from sleeves, collapsible top hats, strings of colored hankies, a touch of hypnotism, communion with the dead—there was a great scramble for seats. Managers and councilmen were denied their usual priorities: no rows reserved for them. So Ruby had to bundle up baby-san an hour early and get in line. Heard the roar from the amphitheatre. Was Mertan manufacturing pigeons or wrestling with his chains? I confess, I've seen his act before. This is his third appearance at Manzanar. Mimi stood over my bed. Did she expect politeness from me? I ignored her. I picked my toes. What was she up to? Why wasn't she disgusted by my dirty feet, my scratchy beard, my general dishevelment and decay?

"Harold."

Didn't say a word.

"Harold."

Scratched my ass.

She sat down on the bed. I moved away. "Harold." Tentatively, shyly, she stroked my cheek. "Harold, you haven't left this room in over a month."

"Been busy," I grumbled, grudging the power of her touch. Skin prickled. Heart boomed. Put my head in her bosom. She stroked some more. Didn't fumble for her breasts. Had no intention of inching toward her crotch. Bumping souls was good enough. I kissed whatever flesh was available. Nose, wrist, ankle. Don't tell me we weren't making love! Genital friction isn't the only kind of music. Let others undress! She kissed my knuckles, I sucked her forearms. We thanked Mertan for granting us an hour. She left right before the end of the magic show.

Somebody at the window in the dead of night, poking here and there, scrubbing the window screen with one fingernail, Mertan back to haunt me maybe, sorry I don't believe in magic, so I ignored the scratching a while, but you know, the sounds weren't frantic, they had a definite melody, *rum, rum, rum,* and I had to find out who was bothering to serenade me in such a way. Gathered up my blanket like Geronimo, stepped over Poleon, walked around Fumi and Mitsuo, ready to greet any face that happened to float across the screen, didn't see a thing. The scratching stopped. Climbed out the window higgledy-piggledy. Dad was sitting on the ground.

"Dad, you come home for good? Should I wake Fumi? We'll have a celebration."

"Bend over," he said, sullen as ever.

So I kneeled, thinking he had something important to say and wanted my face to be level with his. He sprang up, climbed along my spine, put his legs around my shoulders, and told me I'd better rise. I complied. It isn't every day you get the chance to play horse with your own father. "Dad, where you want to go? Inside, outside?"

"Take me on a ride."

I grabbed his ankles, steadied myself and ran, a little

silly, pumping my head like an ostrich. The stars were out. The wind didn't bite. We moved so fast, the barracks went by in a blur. Dad grew imperious. "Lick my shoe."

"I can't."

"Sing to me."

"Can't run and sing at the same time, Dad. My lungs will explode. You want me to die?"

He wouldn't answer. He prodded my poor ribs with his heels. "Faster." Didn't waver, didn't flounce. Carried Dad over territory I had never seen before. Extravagant pear bottoms gaped at us from the trees. Shrubbery shot up to my chest. Felt a tug at my sleeve. Looked down. Poleon was crawling through the thick tropical leaves, his bum exposed, wearing only his spats and his sailor hat. So I stooped for him, a difficult maneuver with Dad on my shoulders, and my knees sank through the leaves, touched the wet ground that gave a little, soft as flesh— who would have believed earth and moss could sweat so much? Poleon climbed aboard, hugging Dad's back with his thighs, and I rose slowly out of the wetness with the two of them on top, and together we were a swaying tower, not very reliable under ordinary circumstances, though here it would have to do. "Don't lean," I warned Napoleon. My neck burned, my biceps twitched. Metal eyes marked my cheeks; Poleon's spats blocked my view. Height was our great advantage. We were taller than most of the trees. Dad fell asleep. Poleon picked pears.

Anchor man, I was left to fight the vegetation, to steer us through the jungle, blind, my knees churning full speed to keep us from being caught in the muck. Were there worms in my socks? Couldn't stop to tell. Thank God, the ground hardened and Poleon saw a clearing straight ahead. He dropped his pears, shook Dad awake, and almost boffed our tower by writhing for all he was worth; his convulsions sent tremors through Dad, and I had to rock and sway like a jib in order to keep up- right and weather the worst of Napoleon's thrusts. "Poleon," I said, dizzy, gulping air, "what's wrong?" Dad moaned, "Let me down, ohhhh." "Shhhh Dad," I said, "we'll make it through." Poleon's writhings grew more regular, and after I got used to his rhythms our pace improved, and pretty soon we were moving faster than ever. Poleon raised one spat, and in spite of the bugs in the air and the swishing ferns I saw the source of his convulsions: Chuichi and Gordon were in the clearing, with Blackstone, Unc' Haraguchi, and a gaggle of old men, bachelors probably, and Uncle's disciples. They all wore convicts' clothes, except Blackstone, who had a long coat, a widebrimmed hat like Wendell's, and trousers with baggy knees and stingy cuffs. What were they doing so close to Manzanar? Were they part of a road gang, attacking the jungle scrub, Blackstone their overseer? Whatever their official occupation, they were jitterbugging in the clearing at a furious rate, without a dance floor, without a band, whizzing partners through the air, making music with hands and tongues, shaking their torsos in perfect syncopation, jiving in the low grass. Chuichi was coupled with Gordon; Blackstone and Sensei were together; the old men interchanged partners among themselves. Was it only foolishness, an elaborate means to trample the grass? I don't care. Eager to join them, to couple up with somebody there, I rocked the tower too hard: Napoleon and Dad tumbled over and rolled in the grass. Poleon was lost. Dad crawled about aimlessly. I tapped Chuichi's shoulder and cut in. Was Gordon annoyed? Did he leer at me? I was too excited to tell. Oh, the dancing we did! Me and Gordon in tune again, like old times, but better, much better, because we weren't colonists now, or miserable Nisei journalists feeding off our futility, and Blackstone no longer had any power over me. Wasn't my jive as good as his? Sensei may have been a formidable partner, the way he combined the snake dance with the jitterbug, but Gordon knew all the latest steps. Clearly the field was ours. The old men paused to watch us. Even Blackstone was impressed. Should I try an entrechat? Gordon, sweetheart, show them all how you wiggle your ass. You the Merry Maid of Manzanar, a cunt inspector in disguise, or are you somebody else? Dad, I'll help you, I will; Poleon stay where you are, I'll find you, only let me finish my dance.

Five

Thursday JULY 2: 1942

Reminders for Today:

Tell Ruby to wash hair.

Fix Napoleon's sailor suit. Hide it from
Mitsuo, he will be mad. Will husband
ever understand Napoleon wants nothing
to do with Boy Scouts? Hints have no
help. Fumiko, you must use firm
persuasion.

Make sure brother interviews Mr Geiger
for paper. Why is Harold such a
nuisance? Does he think everything I say
is for benefit of administration? Lord,
must I be brother's enemy by proxy.
I am not Mitsuo's mouthpiece.

Harold, on my honor, I have nothing to
do with administration. Mitsuo is
manager against my wishes. I do not
believe in politics. If politics could bring
Mother here, I would volunteer to be
manager of all the managers, but not
before.

Must find new way to shake little sister
out of bed. She says, Sis is so Japanesey.
Sis is a crab. Missy, there are some
people around here who are more
crabby than I am. If I am too severe
with her, she will stay out until
midnight to punish me. She is happy if
she knows I will sit up & worry.
Mother, should I have babies when I
have brothers and sisters and husband
to look after? I would never want baby
of mine born and raised in camp.
Beside, I have a baby, Chuichi.
Husband laughs if I say this. But he is
proud of Chuichi just the same.
How many other managers have
brother-in-law who is in USA Army?
Mitsuo is a boaster. "Do you think the
President could win war without my
brother-in-law? He is a machine gunner.

He writes us every day." This is such a
lie. We hardly ever hear from Chuichi
since the war. Once in two three months.
If Chuichi is political asset for Mitsuo
I will not complain. Neighbor next door
wants to know why husband is so pushy
like Jews. Why he orders us around for
administration sake. She thinks Hakujins
pay husband in gold. I tell her husband
make nineteen a month like doctors and
newspapermen. She laughs at me. Says
husband must be crazy to love Hakujins
for nineteen a month. I say not a
question of love & I end conversation.
I do not tell her husband break out in
rash every night. I do not say husband
toss and cry in sleep. Husband is more
afraid of Hakujins than anybody.
Neighbor-san, I do not have to be
philosopher to know why husband
wants to be manager. Insecurity problem
very grave with him, so job of boss man
gives him confidence. Neighbor-san, if I
told you Mother & Father of Mitsuo had
TB & die when he was seven years old,
you will run & tell everybody to look
out, Mitsuo is contagious, lock him up.
You would not stop to think what it

means for boy to be without a family.
So I say nothing to you. Only one
Uncle in America & Uncle very poor
& take out misery on orphan nephew.
Beat him up, starve him, so Mitsuo ran
away. Priests in Salinas found him &
took him to Catholic Charities Home.
He was only Nihonjin boy in Home.
Italian orphans made fun of him & said
yellow face means Mitsuo has urine in
his blood. He found way to survive at
Home. Became yes-man to Italian boys
for ten years. So Neighbor-san, if
husband gives service to Hakujins today
it is not a big surprise. It has become
a habit.

Mr Geiger says I am making much
progress. I am having difficulties with
indefinite articles & punctuation &
arrangement of adjectives, but when I
told him I was the oldest child in big
family & had to help Mother with
babies & it was hard to stay in school,
so I only went up to the third grade,
he told me I shouldn't be ashamed
because I am very good with adverbs.

I wish Harold would listen to me &
write an article about Mr Geiger.

Biggest nuisance in whole world is Dad.
We cannot agree. Dad has taken
advantage of Mother's absence. All his
bad habits have returned. He smokes
in bed & buys saké from Kibei cooks. We
cannot make home respectable. He
says it is too hot during the day & he
cannot bother to wear clothes. He
curses & chases mosquitoes & he must
have his drinking companions. They
are the worst offenders. They have taken
over our little apartment & Ruby is
afraid to be alone with them. They are
smelly old men from Dad's
prefectural society, men with filthy
mouths & filthy ideas. They spit on
our floor & I am expected to clean up for
them & serve them. I have warned
Dad a thousand times. Home is not the
place for such activities. If I chase
the old men out they come back in an
hour & I do not have strength to
fight them every single day. Dad says I
must not shame him in front of his

companions, but I have to take up stern
measures unless he reforms. Dad is
uncivilized.

Napoleon mopey today. He is lonely for
Chuichi. So I have secured uniform
for him in secret. But he must not wear
it when husband is home. Sailor suit
would offend him. Mitsuo recognizes
only one uniform, uniform of his
Boy Scout troop. He was a Boy Scout
at Catholic Home. Boy Scouts
shaped his character, he says, & made
him American. So brother must
keep uniform out of sight. Mother, I am
weary of so many squabbles. Progress
at school is only morale builder. I do not
think I will be able to master definite
article, but I practice every day before &
after laundry hour.

Friday SEPTEMBER 11: 1942

Reminders for Today:

I am a thirty-year-old delinquent.
Must write note to Mr Geiger asking

forgiveness for not coming to class.
Have not made entry in Diary for eleven
days. My grammar will suffer. Dr
Higami recommends famous nerve tonic
for falling out hair & general nervous
disorder, I know results in advance.
Famous tonic is very powerful but
cannot work major miracle. Only one
solution. I would drown myself
tomorrow if I could find a lake. I will
order husband to construct pond for
Block 38, then I will drown myself for
sure. Who will look after
Chuichi???????????

This is the second week I am hiding in
apartment because of shame. I cannot
go outside. Whole camp is aware of
sister's condition. Mitsuo says he must
resign. But he gives no signs of doing
so. His office is as full as ever. I must
carry every burden. If I run to laundry
room, neighbor women will stare.
They will whisper, poor Fumiko, she
knows illegitimate baby cannot be
normal. It will be born without arms.
No, I cannot go outside. Last
Monday Napoleon came in screaming,

Chuichi, Chuichi. He was crazy with
laughing & crying. He danced & hugged
me. I am so used to see him in dreamy
downcast mood with slouchy shoulders &
dull eyes. He clutched my housecoat &
dragged me across the room. "Chuichi,
Chuichi." Napoleon Tanaka, I said,
has someone put the devil inside you? I
cannot leave apartment. If neighbor
women see me, they will laugh at us. But
little brother's madness gave him a
fierce strength impossible to overcome.
He pushed me through the door &
would not even let me hide my face from
neighbors. "Chuichi, Chuichi." A
soldier approached the barracks from
main road. Sun was very bright &
played tricks. Flared behind soldier &
kept him surrounded with haze.
Soldier was not bothered. He walked
through the fire. He had no buttons
or decorations on his coat. His
uniform was filthy & torn. I did not
need to see his face. I recognized
him by his step & his frown was evident
a thousand feet away. Let the devil
take neighbor women! I ran across the
road. Napoleon could not keep up

with me. Chuichi did not wave & I
thought perhaps the sun had
distracted him. I did not want to consider
the condition of his uniform. I gave
myself encouragement. Fumiko, there is
nothing to fear. You are in the middle
of a dream. Men do not walk through fire,
not even Chuichi. But I could not hide
my dread. Darling brother had not come
to us from Georgia on furlough.
Otherwise Army would have notified
WRA & Swann-san would have
capitalized on the event. He would have
brought a band to our door. Also
there would be decorations & buttons. I
kissed Chuichi & took him to the
apartment. I was so very nervous. I
shouted, little sister, come out
from behind your curtain. Chuichi is
here! Lord, how can a person sleep
for twenty hours! I had to wake her.
She barked at me before she would
open her eyes, but when she saw Chuichi
she jumped out of bed half-naked.
She put her head under Chuichi's arm &
cried. Chuichi touched sister's hair
with soft strokes, but his face was still
severe. Without warning he picked

her up with one hand, turned around,
found Napoleon with his other
hand, & began to spin them around the
room. Commotion rocked hurricane
lamp & overturned husband's favorite
chair. Window rattled, floor creaked
under brother's wild step. I wanted to
order him to stop, but sister's giggle &
Napoleon's delight broke his frowns & he
laughed with them. He put them
down & battled with his dizziness.
Napoleon fell down. Sister sat on
her bed. Stay there, I said, & closed the
curtain. Brother & I have important
business. I sent out Napoleon to summon
Harold. Still dizzy, Chuichi said,
Where's Dad? I told him Dad moved out.
His dizziness left & his severity came
back. I did not know what to do.
—Chuichi, it was his own choice. Dad
did not want to live with us. He feels
more comfortable with the old men from
his *kenjinkai*. He is always welcome
here. Chuichi, Napoleon will take you to
see Dad, but I cannot go. Little sister
has shamed us. Dr Higami says evidence
is conclusive. Sister will have baby in
the spring. Harold will not help me. He

will not cooperate with my plan.
Bachelor must be found to marry her.
We will offer money. Harold says,
Jesus Christ, she's only thirteen! Do you
want to saddle her with someone who
picks his nose in public & coughs up
phlegm? I say, Would you prefer sister
marry gangster in zoot suit who will
end up in the electric chair? Harold
shouts, Let her marry me! Chuichi wasn't
listening. He was staring at the folds
in little sister's curtain.

Husband swears Chuichi's sudden
appearance will do him much harm. He
can no longer boast to constituents
about brother-in-law's career in the
Army. "What happened?" he asks.
Chuichi does not like to talk to me about
his days in the Army. I have to go to
Napoleon & Napoleon cannot tell a story
correctly. I ask him, Napoleon, does
brother have discharge papers? He says
no. Army boss gave him a blue card.
—What is the significance of this blue
card? Napoleon smiles. "Sis, blue
card is for boochies! The President is
going to send us one in the mail."

Napoleon says the President visited
Chuichi's camp in Georgia, but
Chuichi was not allowed to see him.
Why not, Napoleon? "Because the
President is afraid of boochies. Didn't he
take Mom away?" Oh Napoleon, what
did Chuichi tell you? "Chuichi says
they took him out of bed & put him in an
old garage & he had to sing My
Country 'Tis of Thee, Sweet Land of
Liberty, until the President left." Oh
what a crazy story! Go outside and play.

I do not care what kind of discharge
Chuichi gets. If Chuichi's presence hurts
husband's political chances, too bad. I
am happy Chuichi is here. Perhaps it is
evil & selfish to say so, but I am glad
about the blue card. Blue card has
brought brother to us.

Monday MARCH 15: 1943
Reminders for Today:

I cannot bear to be with bachelors &
councilmen for another day! I will

— *146* —

beg WRA chiefs to put an end to the
registration. Husband sits in
hospital & I am left with the job of
answer man & nursery maid for whole
block. Councilmen are hopeless.
They sit in Mitsuo's office because they
want to collect councilman's pay,
but they are afraid to pick up a pencil
because of the Blood Brothers. They
moan & shake & start fights with the
bachelors who come to the office a
hundred times a day to change answers &
look for advice. Bachelors are very
vain. They think the entire registration
program revolves around their
whims & if they do not answer the
questionnaires in the right way,
they say they will all be punished.
They swear Mr Swann has already
stolen away a bachelor from another
block. I say, Ridiculous. They
cannot read the questions themselves,
so they have to rely on me &
if I do not chat with them beforehand,
if I fail to ask them about their health,
they ignore the questionnaires and look
the other way. No matter what I do,

they distrust me because of Dad. They
call me Cruel Daughter & even if I
had a statement from Mother about Dad's
tricks, about his great stubbornness,
bachelors would not believe me. They
have a proverb: Daughter who
forsakes father inherits worms. They eye
me with disgust & I am supposed to
serve them with patience & courage while
husband takes long holiday in
hospital. Baa!

I do not tell Ruby, but baby Benjamin
is my only joy. I am not allowed to
touch diapers or play with baby until I
have sister's permission. She is very
bossy. She says, I'm the mother, not you!
Oh, she makes me boil. Sister, who do
you think raised you and Napoleon?
What does she know about babies!
Someone has been bringing presents for
baby Benjamin in the middle of the
night. This morning I opened the
curtain & saw a bassinet. Sister tried
to win me over with her slyness. Where
did it come from? "How should I
know! Maybe I got a fairy godmother."
Yes, a fairy godmother who wears a

zoot suit. Sister, the same bassinet was
stolen from the commissary two
days ago. You must take it back. "No!"
If I argue with her, she says she will
run away with baby.

I cannot stitch family together without
magic thread. Mother is far away.
Dad is my enemy. Husband is no help.
Darling brother has become a No-No.
Kibei have adopted him. He has no time
for me. Oniisan lives in a dream.

Monday DECEMBER 6: 1943

Reminders for Today:

Mitsuo will not give up his duties. He
roams the camp every morning and
inspects the empty barracks. There are
no more children left to hiss at him &
he has enough sense to stay clear of the
bachelor dorm. He is happy for the
first time in a year. He does not want to
leave. Each week the administrative
staff is sliced in half. Only one watchtower is functioning. Mr Swann has

— *149* —

gone to Washington & in spite of what
the Hakujins tell us, I know he will
never be back. There is no future for him
in the WRA. The Allies are winning
the war. —Husband, we cannot stay forever. Baby Benjamin will soon be last
baby in camp. Ruby will not find a suitor
here. We must go to Chicago. The
Hakujins have warned us. Camp will be
closed in July. Mitsuo has jitters
whenever I mention word Chicago.
"Fumi, it is not safe for us to be on
the outside. American soldiers on leave
think of murder if they see a Japanese
face." Husband, half of Manzanar yogore
are in Chicago. I have not heard
reports of murder. He will not listen. He
says Hakujins have made him care-
taker of the camp. He must watch over
the barracks until all the yogore come
back.

Saddest case of all is Oniisan. He sits in
tiny apartment all day, makes up
songs & has conversations with baby
Benjamin. Until today I have never
heard a grown man tell a baby about

philosophy! Does he want to poison baby's mind? If only Mr Geiger was here! He would scold him for such talk.

Wednesday JUNE 7: 1944

Reminders for Today:

"Dad, this is your last chance! I won't ask you again. Are you coming?" I went through trouble of getting leave clearance for him so we could go to Chicago as one family, but what does Dad care! He is happy in this ghost camp, with the diseased old men from his prefecture who have become scavengers and loiterers. "Are you coming?" He spit on the ground for an answer, crazy father with a rotten heart and empty head. Finally he looked up. "Where's Chuichi?" I wanted to shake sense into him, but just touch him & I would never get out of the dormitory alive. Those old men are so vicious! "Dad, has Chuichi visited

you lately? You know he's been in Tule
over a year."

"Then I won't go with you."

Mom would have fixed him. She would
have dragged him around the
dormitory by his ears until he agreed
to go. The old fools were already
crowded around me, sympathizers for
Dad in unwashed pajamas, I could
tell what was on their minds: Cruel
Daughter, Cruel Daughter. It
wasn't safe to be there. So I left Dad
our Army blanket & the remains of
Mitsuo's canned goods, reached over &
kissed him. He made an awful
face & wiped the kiss away. "Good-by,
Dad."

Diary, you are my one friend. Only you
know how hard I worked to make
Mitsuo leave camp. Lectures from the
new leave officer about golden
opportunities in Chicago meant nothing
to him. When I said, Husband, I have
leave clearance for whole family, you can
stay or go, whatever you wish, he
didn't believe me. But when big trunk

from Montgomery Ward arrived, he
said, "Fumi, don't leave me here alone.
The bachelors will murder me."
Husband began to pack.

Little sister is still obstinate. She says
we must transport Benjamin's bassinet
to Chicago or she will not budge
from the spot. Little brother walks
through camp in a dream, believing
one day Chuichi will emerge from the
eye of a dust storm & save us from
the Hakujins. Napoleon, I will ask
weather man in Chicago to
manufacture dust storm special for you.
Perhaps Chuichi will show up there.
With much persistence I have cured
husband, sister & little brother of
dreaded immobility. We will have a
happy life in Chicago. We will
forget the scars of war. We will not
congregate too closely with Nihonjin
community. We will not give people
opportunity to say: Japs are dangerous,
Japs are unclean, Japs always stick
together. Oniisan disapproves of my
program. He will not come with us.

He would rather rot here with Dad.
Tomorrow, after we leave, he will move
in with the bachelors & in another
year the dust & the wind will turn him
into stone.

Six

Across the shower room in pillowcase masks we ran shouting our little song. *No sep-a-ray-shun of fac-il-it-ees. This is Japan. Men and women bathe together.* Taro slapped the hands that reached for the towel rack. Shrieks and bumping bodies didn't bother Grandma Odo. She kept her grin throughout the panic. She threw a bar of soap at me. *You Hokoku*gangsters!* Taro was eager to throttle her. I pushed him out. *I take my orders from Tosh*, he said, *not you.*

Gordon made a whimper under his mask—it was twisted around. The eye holes were in the back of his head. He stumbled. Sitting on his knees he pulled off the mask, stuffed it inside his shirt, and vomited. *Chuichi, no more missions for me. I will write speeches for Ho-*

* Hokoku Seinen-dan: Young Men's Organization to Serve Our Mother Country.

koku and *Hoshi-dan*,* but *I can't go on frightening naked women.*

Wipe your mouth, Taro said. *That old witch will send the Army after us. I should have put her out of her misery.*

Taro rebuked us at Hokoku headquarters. *Tosh, these two are the wrong men for a raiding party. This one puked and that one wouldn't let me take care of my business.*

I know, Gordon said. *Strangling grandmothers is your specialty.*

Taro's razor was out, so I picked up a chair. Toshio put his arm around me and took me outside.

I am Toshio's number-one bodyguard and strongarm boy, and Taro is his hatchet man. Tosh is grand master of Hokoku. Grandma Odo calls us Jap stormtroopers. She has contempt for our bugles and our head bands and our gray sweatshirts with the emblem of the rising sun. Grandma is the head of our rival, the Nippon Service Club. She loves the Emperor as fervently as Toshio, but she hates General Tojo and his war party. She hates all soldiers, American and Japanese. We have beaten up Grandma's friends and relatives, we have threatened the Christian ministers who support the Nippon Service Club, we have raided the women's shower room a dozen times a month, but Grandma's grins will ruin me.

* Sokuji Kikoku Hoshi-dan: Organization to Return Immediately to the Homeland.

A bat colony lives in the eaves of our dormitory. Taro is afraid of bats. They wrap themselves inside their winged fingers and sleep most of the day. You can see rows and rows of them hanging upside down from the eaves. At dusk they unfurl themselves and begin to screech. That's when Taro gets the spooks. The bats flutter and dart about the roof but never collide. Taro says the bats have evil designs. He won't go near the dorm alone after dark. He thinks the bats will break through the screen door while we're asleep, bite our necks, and grow fat on our blood. I caught a bat. It must have been sleepy. It tumbled from its perch just before dinnertime, crashed into the dormitory wall, and dazed itself. I put the bat in Taro's bed.

Taro was a barber's apprentice before evacuation. Now he shaves the heads of Hokoku strongarm boys. Our ceremonial haircuts are supposed to make us good warriors and give us *Yamato damashii*, Japanese fighting spirit. I don't need Grandma Odo to remind me how foolish we are with our shorn scalps. All I have to do is look at the bumps on Gordon's head. Taro taunted Wendell. *This one has a knife and never uses it. I asked for cadres, and what does Tosh give me?*

Mother, Wendell said, *you crazy. I don't cut up children. The blade stays in my pocket. I'm going to sleep.* Taro sat on his bed and lectured us on the ways and means of discouraging all children from joining the Nippon Service Club. *Grandma must be crushed.* His lecture woke the bat. The sheet began to move. Taro kicked the mattress. The bat walked out from under the sheet, using its fingertips to steer. Taro screamed, and the bat darted up into the rafters making little noises. Taro's eyes followed the bat. *Who put the creature in my bed?*

I expected his razor. He sat down and cried. The bat's shadow flickered on the ceiling. *Chuichi, we will all be dead by morning.* I opened the door and picked up a stone, took careful aim, fired, and brought the bat plummeting down. Taro shuddered and looked away as I picked it up and threw it outside. Hiroshi was near the door. *What's going on? Reverend Tajiri has been talking against us. Tosh wants him silenced.* Taro sneered at me. We put on our masks.

Reverend Tajiri's teeth chattered. Hiroshi trapped him behind his altar. We didn't have to say boo. The congregation ran out of the church squealing when they saw our masks. Gordon slapped the Reverend's secretary and told him to shut up, but he couldn't prevent his own knees from shaking. Taro held his razor near the Reverend's gullet. *Christian scum. A Jap camp is not the place for your Jesus. If you make one more speech against our friends in Hokoku, I will carve your face like a pumpkin and slaughter you on your own Communion table. Get out of Tule Lake.*

Master, I will pack tonight.

Wendell kicked the pews in the Reverend's tiny

church. He ran out waving his arms and screeching like a bat. Hiroshi wouldn't let us go. *Brothers, this visit was only a preliminary. We have work to do for Hoshi-dan.*

The elders were worried about Barrack 9. The oldest sons in two families refused to renounce their American citizenship and failed to ask for a place on the next exchange boat to Japan. Hiroshi, we don't need a whole shock troop to frighten one barrack. Me and Taro are horrible enough. Take Wendell and Gordon to the canteen. My treat.

I'm staying with you, Gordon said.

So the three of us went to intimidate the two oldest sons. Shuzo Nakamura begged us not to harm his old father and his baby sisters. Taro slapped him and shaved his head. *Now you are one of us. We do not tolerate traitors in Hokoku. Do not speak to me of American citizenship. We are prisoners of war. Your papa and your sisters will serve the mother country.* Next, we tweaked the ears of the entire Okuma family. Gordon did not waver once. *Good boy*, Taro said. *We'll turn you into a soldier in spite of yourself.*

You could hear the lowing of the bulls—hungry, afraid of the dark?—from the camp farm. And the smell of cow shit, always powerful in the dorm, was strongest at night when you weren't busy and you did most of your thinking with your nose. Hiroshi had stories to tell. Tonight, for the tenth time, he recounts his adventures as a houseboy for a fading twenty-five-year-old starlet in Pismo Beach. *Once I got so dizzy I mistook an armpit for a crotch and fucked it to death.* Wendell grows pale while Hiroshi relives each of the starlet's requests. Hiroshi demands a story from Gordon in return, and soon the evening will be somber. Not because Gordon is in a particularly bitter mood, but no matter what story Hiroshi pries out of him—why the Earth will explode in five thousand years, whether or not plants can think, the geometry of the stars, the trials and tribulations of fruit-stand workers in and around LA—Gordon will end up talking about Manzanar; he'll leak out words of Hal, feuds with Beardsly, editorial disputes with Swann, and the three of us, Hiroshi, Wendell, and me, forced to listen, to remember, will fidget, poke our fingers through the holes in our masks, our faces growing rigid, until Hiroshi gets up and says, *I have to go on an errand for Tosh.* You see, memory's an evil word. Strongarm boys, we have purged ourselves of humanness for the moment. Taro alone finds pleasure in Gordon's stories. He isn't from Manzanar. He's from Minidoka, where the men are wild and cruelty is in their nature.

I was late for morning exercises. Taro woke me with a kick. *Fool, the bugles have been braying for an hour.* I brought out my ceremonial sword. My pupils stood at ease on the main firebreak. Joshi-dan* girls, Hokoku volunteers, old ladies in sun hats, kindergarteners, Issei

* Hokoku Joshi Seinen-dan: Young Women's Organization to Serve Our Mother Country.

bachelors, married men, and married women. I am Ho-koku drillmaster for Blocks 7 through 12. Last night's conversion must have taken hold. Shuzo Nakamura's gleaming head was in the vanguard. His baby sisters were with him. They both held miniature Jap flags. I un-sheathed the sword and began the drill. *Atsumare*, I shouted, and my pupils fell into place. We faced the rising sun and paid homage to the Emperor. I try, but I can't get accustomed to drilling in Japanese, with sword in hand. Toshio says this is the only way to instill *Yamato damashii*. He has practiced the commands with me. *Hocho tore*, and my pupils become goosesteppers. *Bango*, and they count off. *Tsuke ken*, and they pretend to fix bayonets. Sometimes I slip and bark an order in Army English. Hiroshi or Taro is always there to correct me. *Wash-sho! Wash-sho!* The guards in the towers watch us with amusement. The Issei bachelors come hobbling out of their dormitory; *Yamato damashii* cures their lumbago once they reach the firebreak. The Joshi-dan girls are ruthless marchers. They put the strongarm boys to shame. Without Grandma Odo we would have had a perfect morning.

Grandma's legion of twelve- and thirteen-year-olds stood in their knickers on the edge of the firebreak and sang Japanese hymns while we marched and drilled. My buglers couldn't drown them out. With a yardstick Grandma mimicked my swordsmanship and parodied my military calls. The guards leaned out of their towers to applaud her. *See*, Taro said to Wendell. *I told you to take care of those brats. I will murder them all in their sleep.* He shook his fist at Grandma. *Baya, you will live to regret your jamborees and your wooden swords.* Oh Grandma, I didn't mind. Your mimicry deserved our applause too. I saw myself in each one of your moves. I wanted to laugh out loud. Taro might have turned his razor on me, but that's not what stopped me. Had I guffawed during the drill and allowed my pupils to look at you, they would have discovered for themselves the empty pomp of the morning exercises, and Toshio would have been compromised. So I held the laughter in. Grandma, you caught the arch of my back, the way I have of licking my index finger when I'm anxious or bored, the stiffness of my neck, my hesitancy, the true hatred I have for my sword. I'm sorry.

I miss Dad. Mother always acted so superior to him. She said the *baishakunin* tricked her into coming to America. She does not want to remember that her own uncle arranged the marriage, that even if her great-great-great-grandfather was a samurai warrior, even if she came from a Tokyo *ken* and graduated from women's college, and Dad's ancestors were poor Osaka fishermen, her family was starving in Tokyo. *Chuichi, I did not love your father. Not for one day. The baishakunin swore father was an important farmer with land in the valleys of Sacramento, and he did not own an acre. He was a common day laborer, and I was a picture bride with a college certificate.* Mother, you told us Dad did not love us, that he cared only for saké and the old friends of his society, but how much love did we ever show for Dad? We saw him through your eyes. He pulled my nose, yes, he tweaked my ears when I was nine and ten, he never gave pennies to Harold or me, he threatened to abandon us, to beat us, after a drunken rage; but Mother, do ogres play goh, do they laugh with friends, do they cry, do they have crippled fingers, a sunken chest? Gordon and I went for a walk.

Chuichi, will the government expect me to fight against the Americans? I would like to work with children or repair the cities that have been bombed. Should I become a doctor's aide? One thing, I am through with journalism.

He was leaving for Japan in twenty days, and he was blue because we would not be going together.

Gordon, perhaps you can be Unc' Haraguchi's bodyguard. This made him laugh. Why? Don't you think the Emperor will make him an ambassador?

An ambassador at least. I'm not quarreling with that. But Sensei is world famous for his nepotism. He will want to save the job of bodyguard for Wendell.

Impossible. Wendell is scheduled to be with Toshio and me on the last exchange boat. We might be here for five more years.

I know. He was blue again.

We came upon an open-air debate. Grandma Odo was

teamed with Reverend Tajiri against the board of elders of Hoshi-dan. They sat in camp chairs on the outdoor stage. Unc' Haraguchi spoke for the elders. Grandma Odo wagged her head at him. She wore a kimono under her Navy coat. The elders must have incensed her. It was the only time I ever saw her without a grin. *Shame, old men who speak for violence.* She had a conference with Tajiri.

Gordon put his head in his hands. *Chuichi, let's pray for the Reverend. Wasn't he supposed to jump camp? If the hatchet man finds out, it'll be curtains. Taro, wherever you are right now, please stay away. Chuichi, should we give the Reverend a friendly warning? My mask is in my coat pocket. I'll take it out. He'll get the idea.*

Gordon, no mask waving. We can't interrupt the debate. If the elders don't murder us, Grandma will.

Grandma tongue-lashed the elders. They squeezed their shoulders together and hung their heads. *It is fortunate for you that I am a woman of peace. Otherwise I would break your foolish old bones. Did the Emperor ask for war? What can you expect when generals become prime ministers? We will not serve the Emperor while the Imperial Army and Navy sit in command. Wicked ones, you would accomplish nothing without your Hokoku gangsters.*

Gordon and I shrank with shame. Only Unc' Haraguchi was strong enough to withstand Grandma. *Crazy*

*hag, bring a plague to the white faces, not to us. We
did not send you to a concentration camp. I praise our
young Hokoku brothers who have sworn eternal devo-
tion to Nihon, who are the Emperor's priests in America.*

We sucked on fudgsicles at the coöp. The manager
offered to give them to us for free. *Go away,* Gordon
said. *I pay for what I buy. Chuichi, there is only one
solution. I will become the Emperor's bootblack.
Shouldn't the Divine One have the privilege of experi-
encing one of my fabulous spit shines before he dies?*

Gordon, no good. The Emperor does not wear shoes.
How do you know?

Toshio was waiting for us in the dorm. Gordon and I
had no doubts about our target for tonight. The slap-
slap of Taro's razor gave me the chills. Tosh, I can
handle this alone. The Reverend was only coaching
Grandma. I'll punish him. I'll give him a wallop he won't
forget. I'll pack his trunk, escort him to the main gate,
and make sure he gets a ticket to Manzanar or Jerome.
Chuichi, Tosh said, *put on your mask.*

Gordon, when I was in Manzanar, sitting on my tail
all day waiting for my redemption to arrive in a brown
envelope from the President, saying Chuichi Albert
Tanaka, we have made a grave error, you are not a Jap,
Toshio came to me. I laughed at his ceremonial coat and
his bald head. I knew he was a Kibei troublemaker. I
shouted at him. Bastard, it's because of you and your
Jap sympathizers that I'm here. I'm a soldier. I don't

belong in a Jap camp. I threatened to beat him with a stick. He was quiet. He didn't move. Are you deaf? Look at my hands. I've been trained to kill. I raised my hand. He smiled. *Brother*, he said, *Uncle Sam has done a job on you. Your rehabilitation will take us a little while. But your disease is not so uncommon. I promise you. In a month's time you won't want to be Yankee Doodle Dandy.*

The church was locked. Taro slashed the window screen, climbed in, and opened the door for us. He called softly into the dark of the church, *Here Reverend, here Reverend.* The pearl handle of his razor had an unnatural shine. *Here Reverend.* Wendell lit a match. Reverend was hiding in the corner, a black coat over his head. He didn't squeal when Toshio withdrew the coat. He sat in his pew like a dazzled cat.

In Watsonville I danced on the roofs and plucked bats out of the air for Farmer Shikuma. He swore they hexed his strawberries and frightened customers away. I didn't believe a word, but he did set a fair price: a nickel a bat. On a roof, your head high, you stare and stare until you see a puckered face between leaves lit up like diamonds, you shake the tree with a pole, you hoot, you scream, you stamp your feet, and when the bats tumble you have to know how to leap or else the wings only graze your fingers and you're liable to fall.

Blood dribbled on Taro's sleeve. He sliced Reverend's cheeks with quick strokes of his wrist. His elbow never moved. I could have stopped him. Was it Toshio's presence that held me back? I saw the blood, I heard the screams, we all did. Taro's calm, the delicate motion of his hand tricked me. I thought the razor was caressing Tajiri's face.

There was no wind to battle, no moon to make us visible: only night sounds and the puttering of tower guards. Toshio couldn't have seen my trembling jaws, couldn't have heard the short gasps of my breathing, yet he touched me twice. Did he feel the tremor beneath the rough cloth of my field jacket? We ran together, hands clasped, dodging searchlights, and I thought, Tosh, I have threatened little boys in knickers, I have destroyed Fourth of July celebrations at Manzanar and Tule, I have cautioned schoolgirls to give up the lindy hop, I have kicked, slapped, and punched Kibei from Topaz and Minidoka who tried to test your authority, but I won't go near the church again.

Chuichi, the white men have the weapons. We have only the limited use of fear. If the inu did not fear us, we would soon be despised. No better than Boy Scouts.

I dream of Grandma Odo: in her great Navy coat, buttoned to the top, hands in her pockets, chin down, she haunts me while I run. Grandma, how many times have I stood in a crowd, my shirt pulled over my nose, my Hokoku insignia covered, and listened to your harangues? Fascinated, alarmed, when you attacked the blind fury and terror of Hokoku and Hoshi-dan, I was like an eager little boy aroused by the thought of his own transgressions. Grandma, didn't you know that your hold on me was at least as powerful as Tosh's?

Can you stand around, mask in your pocket, dust in your nose from the Reverend's pews, and rub the wooden flanks of Sleepy Anne, the canteen's super pin-ball machine, the girl with electric boobs, can you pull Anne's plunger and watch the steel ball roll through the maze and count your score on the blinking red and blue lights, can you help the ball along with one eye on the tilt sign, can you curse Anne properly and ignore the old men near the stove who are afraid to look at you, Hokoku warrior—do they think I have come to pull their beards in the name of the elders of Hoshi-dan? —without seeing your own torn cheeks on the grimy surface of Anne's glass cover, without seeing blood flow in rivulets under the chipped glass and chase the steel ball to the end of the maze?

The corporals were rough on poor Anne. They pushed me against the scoreboard and frisked me while the tilt sign blinked in my face and Anne's electric boobs blushed with a flurry of sparks. They pulled out my pockets, banged my shins, and dragged me to their jeep. I punched the biggest corporal in the nose. I lost a tooth. More corporals appeared. Their billies flicked in the air. The jeep ride was fun. I didn't feel the kicks. The breeze cooled the blood on my lips. A white orderly came with patches and mercurochrome. My pockets were still hanging out. *Captain, we caught him with the goods.* They dangled my mask. *Don't he look scary with his Jap hood? Should we drown him, Mr. Lovelady?*

Tosh, won't go near that church again, won't go near that church. I'm afraid the Reverend's been sorely used. He was more concerned for my cuts and bruises than for his own bandaged face. It wasn't Hokoku terror that told him to say, *I don't know this boy*, when the corporals made me put on the mask. Compassion's a better word if you dare use it.

The corporals didn't care. It was the stockade for me. *Cool off, bub.* Thirty men in a room without windows. Some had shaved heads like me. Hokoku brothers from another block? Who knows the number of Nihon patriotic societies there are at Tule? Each with its own corps of buglers. We'd much rather squabble among ourselves than fight the Hakujins. There were sniggers when I sat down, and two men spat near my feet. Something sparkled in their hands: they were the masters of the dungeon with their smuggled shards of glass. *Bodyguard to the devil! Hokoku scum!* Taunts alone wouldn't have made me stir. Their spit was a little too close. They hopped and sang and called me sir, with their arms twisted behind their backs. The shards are in my pocket now.

I envied some of them. They managed to sleep all day in that foul room, alive with swarms of gnats, while our bodies blazed like furnaces. I got rid of sweatshirt, boots, and underpants. My neighbor was an old man with chapped lips who sat by himself and shivered. I brought him water in a tin. Did my drooping prick offend him? I'm sorry. I saw the zeal in his eyes. I stepped back. He had come from Manzanar, this old man, Ifukube the fanatic, who broke with the elders of Hoshi-dan, who had no love for Hokoku or interest in our morning exercises, and was picked up on his way to the Hakujin barracks with a torch in his hand and a bottle of gasoline in his pocket. Would he bite me? Grab my twig? He drank the water. He kissed my hands.

Twigs, twigs, what's your predicament when your father is a wandering Jap barber with clippers, razors, and dark green bottles of hair tonic in a leather case but without a shop of his own? Did he enjoy lathering the flabby faces of Hakujin bankers on Main Street? Would they murder him if his razor slipped? I sharpened his scissors for him, I packed his leather case, making sure the bottles were capped tight, I memorized the consistency of that green goo and dreamed of spilling it on my own head, I worried about Dad every time he left the house, because Mom said, *What kind of man is it who works among white filth? Wash your hands before you eat! You've come home with the stink of the Hakujins! One day they will take you and auction off your blood.* How could I deal with subtrahends and minuends, mend the ribs of my kite, or build model bat-

— *170* —

tleships, without thinking of Dad, without seeing his blood in a Hakujin bottle?

Tosh, I said a prayer to the Emperor tonight. I begged him to purify me, to take the taint of America out of my blood. I growled at the schoolgirls last week, I dared them organize another lindy hop, but what would you say if I told you that in the middle of dismantling their loudspeaker I had to resist the desire to dance with the girls, to swing them over my shoulder, to bounce them off my hip—that's the kind of knave I am. I had a white girl in Modesto before the war. She was in love with my green suspenders and my alligator shoes. I might have been Chuichi at home, but in the street I was Yellow Mike, who preferred his meat a little light, who couldn't believe Nisei girls even owned a cunt, who wore brass knucks for show, who boogie-woogied with the best at the Modesto Palace, who wanted to leave Japtown to fight for America and see the world. The corporals let me go.

Chuichi. Wake up.

Lord, I have only been away from the barracks for two days. Can a boy grow wrinkles on his face and develop a twitch in so short a time? Wendell, what's wrong? Has Taro been after you with his razor? Don't he know Chuichi's back?

Gordon's dead. He bumped his head and killed himself. Outside the canteen. He's there now. The Hakujins are coming to get him.

I didn't have time to lace my boots. I ran out in my underpants.

Chuichi, he was laughing when I left him. I only went inside for a Baby Ruth. Gordon's going to bring baseball to Japan. That's why we were laughing so. I said, Can you imagine a bunch of boochies swinging a bat? And when I came out with the Baby Ruth, he was banging his head against the wall. There were boochies standing by, and they didn't do nothing but watch. He moved his head so quick, he got sprayed with his own blood. He had to blink but he didn't stop banging. I said, Gordon, Gordon, don't do that. He jumped off the porch. A jeep was coming through. The soldier bumped his horn, and he wasn't going fast. Gordon dove into the side of the jeep. I heard the smack. His brains flew up in the air.

Wendell cleared a path for me. He said *Hokoku*, and people moved. Those who didn't hear he batted with his elbow, and pointed to the rising sun on his chest. The driver stood over Gordon, hand on holster. His jeep was idling. The windshield was splattered with gore. He'd covered Gordon with a tarp. He was terrified. He couldn't take his eyes off the tarp and put on that grim, mechanical face the Hakujins wear especially for us. *I'm sorry*, he said. *Awfully sorry. He ran into me. I didn't see him.* Then the riot squad arrived on foot, kicking up dust, with their canisters of tear gas on display. Men in gas masks with goggles and bouncing hose that went from shoulder to neck—we'd have thought they were from Mars if they hadn't come around so regularly. The driver's demeanor changed automatically. I wasn't surprised. *Jap fuckers,* he sneered. He aimed his pistol at Wendell and me. *I had to hold these monkeys in line.* He stooped to pull off the tarp. *That crazy bastard rammed right into me. Gonna take an hour to wipe off his mess.* Children shrieked and turned away, but Gordon's dead body wasn't really so gruesome. His knees were curled; his palms were up; and there was a dark corolla of clotted blood where his scalp had been. I jumped. The long fingers caressing my neck didn't belong to Wendell. Like a spook, Taro appeared behind me and whispered in my ear. *We'll avenge him, Chuichi. Hakujin blood will flow as freely as lemonade.* The soldiers wrapped Gordon's body in the tarp and carried it to the jeep; the tear-gas canisters clanked at their sides.

The elders of Hoshi-dan have put Gordon's broken head to good use. Tosh was overruled. The elders have declared a holiday in honor of Gordon and are going to have a public ceremony on the main firebreak. Any Jap caught working on this day can expect the combined wrath of Hokoku and Hoshi-dan. The elders have also demanded that the driver be charged with negligence and murder. Taro's preparing a eulogy. All raids have been suspended until after the ceremony, and Taro sits on his bed sniffling, his eyes bleary and red, putting encomiums in his notebook. It isn't hypocrisy, I can vouch for that. It's very simple. Taro can't love you before you're dead.

I'm against the holiday. I told Toshio. Please don't let Hoshi-dan turn Gordon's death into a political show. We killed Gordon, not the Hakujins. Tule was not the right place for him. I begged him not to go on any raids. He said all he ever wanted to be was a strongarm boy. *Chuichi*, Tosh said, *I cannot disobey Hoshi-dan.*

We Hokoku strongarm boys tapped nails into the ends of broomsticks and cleaned up the firebreak with our paper stabbers, while the industrious Joshi-dan girls carried lumber and stones for miles and built a ceremonial arbor. Hokoku electricians set a loudspeaker on the roof of the arbor; carpenters made a bench in the arbor for the elders to sit on. Our buglers played patriotic songs all morning. And now Chusha the drummer boy goes from door to door, his loud booms a good reminder. It isn't necessary; people stream out of the barracks, sunshine on their solemn faces. See, the firebreak is filling up. I should be up front with the honor guard, not on my knees stabbing candy wrappers, raking dust. The Buddhist priests hog the area around the arbor and refuse to sit down. It's an oversight; no one has brought mats for them. The elders are already inside. A meddler from the Office of Information showed up in a jeep, a camera hanging from his neck. Doesn't he know the Hakujins have been barred from the ceremony by a special Hoshi-dan decree? Three strongarm boys pulled him out of his jeep, broke his camera, and dragged him along the ground. They happened to come my way. I put the Hakujin back in his jeep, started the motor for him, and banged on the roof. Scat!

There was an eruption inside the arbor. The elders rocked the bench, gestured at the crowd, stamped their feet, and pushed one another. Only the Joshi-dan girls standing nearby prevented the arbor walls from falling in. We all turned our heads in the direction of the elders' frantic gestures. Oh Grandma, you should have stayed away. The purple and gold banners of the Nippon Service Club flew over one corner of the firebreak. Grandma Odo had a chorus, a color guard, buglers, and a procession of little boys, come to scrap the dreams of Hoshi-dan. One elder, swollen with rage, screeched into the microphone. The Hakujins must have sabotaged our sound equipment. I heard a prolonged buzz. I didn't let Taro's darting head out of sight. I knew where he was going. Grandma, did you think Taro would let you undo the ceremony before he delivered his eulogy? I threw away the paper stabber and ran after Taro. He pulled down the banner, pushed aside the little boys, and leaped on Grandma. She walked about ten feet without giving up her famous grin, Taro's hands on her throat, his legs around her middle in a scissors hold, then collapsed, Taro riding on top of her. He punched her and screamed. *You dare desecrate our ceremony. You dare defile the memory of one of our warriors.* He got up and began kicking her in the head. Grandma's eyes closed, and her grin, now a pained grimace, held in spite of her split lips and the blood spurting from her nose. I grabbed Taro's head, twisted it, and drove it into the ground. On my knees, laboring with Taro's head, pushing, grunting, fending off the nervous thrusts of his body, I heard the canisters pop. The explosions were soft and didn't hurt my ears. Then the shrillness came—a whistle blasted across the firebreak—and broke my hold on Taro. Gasmask hose, swollen and twisted, squirmed around me. The old men screamed and ran for cover. The dull thud of military policemen's clubs sounded everywhere. Tosh fell, his forehead cracked. I ran toward him, hose brushing my neck, blows glancing off my back. Nothing hurt. I began to cough. The Joshi-dan girls had one policeman stranded near the entrance of the arbor. They tore off his gas mask and his clothes, scratched him, bit him too. Trained in riot tactics, the policeman protected his balls. The arbor came tumbling down on top of the girls. Uncle Haraguchi stood still in the thick of things, while the clubs flailed on both sides of him, gathered up his ceremonial robes, and chanted eerie, frightening curses at the policemen in a singsong voice. The other elders who were still on their feet crouched behind him. I waded into battle, avoiding the outstretched bodies, careful not to step on hands or toes, looking for Tosh. Uncle's chants gave me courage. My eyes burned, and I couldn't swallow. Was that Wendell with his knife out, slashing the thin air? I must have immobilized a policeman. I had a gas mask in my hand. The hose was disconnected, the goggles were twisted out of shape. I put it on. Were the policemen confused? Why was I on the ground? My prick was out, lolling in the grass. Gentlemen, officers of the law, I have to pee. Groggy, all I could think about were bats. I crashed through trees. Napoleon's face was under the leaves. Didn't he recognize me? Brother, don't cry. I never wanted to be a warrior. I got up, took off the mask, and went back into battle.